The Guardians

The Guardians

An Inevitable Destiny

CHARLOTTE DANCISIN

THE GUARDIANS
AN INEVITABLE DESTINY

Copyright © 2019 Charlotte Dancisin.

All rights reserved. No part of this book may be used or reproduced by any means, graphic, electronic, or mechanical, including photocopying, recording, taping or by any information storage retrieval system without the written permission of the author except in the case of brief quotations embodied in critical articles and reviews.

This is a work of fiction. All of the characters, names, incidents, organizations, and dialogue in this novel are either the products of the author's imagination or are used fictitiously.

iUniverse books may be ordered through booksellers or by contacting:

iUniverse
1663 Liberty Drive
Bloomington, IN 47403
www.iuniverse.com
1-800-Authors (1-800-288-4677)

Because of the dynamic nature of the Internet, any web addresses or links contained in this book may have changed since publication and may no longer be valid. The views expressed in this work are solely those of the author and do not necessarily reflect the views of the publisher, and the publisher hereby disclaims any responsibility for them.

Any people depicted in stock imagery provided by Thinkstock are models, and such images are being used for illustrative purposes only.
Certain stock imagery © Thinkstock.

ISBN: 978-1-4917-7120-4 (sc)
ISBN: 978-1-5320-7587-2 (hc)
ISBN: 978-1-4917-7119-8 (e)

Library of Congress Control Number: 2015920836

Print information available on the last page.

iUniverse rev. date: 05/29/2019

In a small store in Pittsburgh, Pennsylvania, a young woman goes into labor. She is rushed to a hospital nearby. Doctors and nurses crowd around the young mother in pain as she begins feeling the ultimate urge to push. The staff quickly preps her for delivery. They shuttle her and the unborn baby into a delivery room, where there are many bright white lights. She screams in pain as her labor grows more intense. Her husband enters the room fully gowned, quickly taking his place at her side. He holds her hand. The young mother sits up to push for what she hopes is that one last time. Then the child is born.

The doctor says to the young couple, "It's a girl!" The young couple rejoice as they hear her first cries.

In another part of the world outside the recesses of Castle Angelica, a statue of a grotesque figure, standing stoic on the steps of a mausoleum, begins to crack as the echoes of a child's cry are heard throughout the kingdom. Finally, a dark figure emerges abruptly from the stone, hungry.

It's those ever-fleeting moments when it seems that nothing you do, nothing anyone else can do for you, will ever satisfy you. You have that "been there, done that" attitude, and through no fault of your own, you have seen and been through too much in your life so that nothing is as pleasurable as it used to be. Not food, not the beautiful home you have built for yourself since your impending divorce, not the thoughts of falling in love, not even sex.

Sex for the most part used to be exciting and exhilarating, waking up every sense of your soul. Now, reaching a climax is how high an octave you can achieve faking it for the sake of having this poor individual on top of you working his ever loving ass off to please you. Really you are merely saving the poor man a pulled muscle—or worse, a bruised libido.

I walk down the street to my car as I do daily on my way to work. My wandering eye catches so many men looking in my direction. Sure, I am good looking, but please stop looking. I am damaged goods. I have been beaten down by life itself, too many long nights up wondering what in the hell have I done waking up next to … argh! The thought of that guy, flashing momentarily back to that ungodly image of sweaty, gluttonous, hairy, snoring! It is reminiscent of a foghorn in the middle of a thick, dense fog in which there is no end in sight giving multiple—no, unwavering warnings to ships in the deep sea of land ahead! Argh! It gives me shivers all over again!

That one is definitely the one where fathers tell their sons. I get an image in my mind of a father sitting in a chair, towering over son and wagging a finger at him, as he is about to send the son off to the big bad world alone. "Son, if you wake up next to a sasquatch, gnaw your own arm off to save yourself from waking her up on your way out the door! Ha! The man has a huge, dirty, cigar-smoking, worn T-shirt, with a belly hanging out. Dad laughs his way back to his worn-out recliner, reaching for his beer and remote. *Wow, what an image! Gotta snap outta that one!* I guess that's what happens when men get comfortable: they get dirty and slobbish! I smile a little and look up to see the street ahead, always aware of my surroundings.

I feel as though I am so damaged, between my childhood traumas and my abandonment issues. Of course, I don't know any girl who doesn't have a daddy issue, and then there is my all-time favorite, my own insecurities due to a piece of shit who would rather screw some whore than his wife. Yeah, and that lonely, broken-hearted wife was me. That is why I am divorced. Well, truthfully I am finally in the process of achieving my divorce now.

I peer ahead, looking for the opportunity to cross the busy street to get into my car and begin this day, much like all the others. People and cars blend together to become a gigantic blur. I give you my life.

I place my iPod on high, blasting Iggy's song "Black Widow." I'm not stomping, just walking with purpose, pissed off at all the time I wasted.

Chapter 1

My cell phone rings in my desk drawer, and I quickly reach over to silence it. Too late—of course everyone is looking in my direction now. I flash an uncomfortable smile, silence the phone, and put it back, but not before I look to see who called. It was him. I don't talk about him. He had put a spring in my step. Why is he calling me now, after all this time has passed? I can feel a smile begin to form on my face, breaking into a huge grin. Damn, I've been had! She saw! *And here she comes*, I think to myself, still smiling.

My best friend and coworker, Jeannie, slides over toward me whispering, "So, um, what's up, Chester Cheetah?"

I smile in spite of myself. "That obvious, huh?"

"Oh yeah, baby, oh yeah!"

"I will tell you when we are done with this meeting, okay?" I whisper, trying not to attract any more attention.

Jeannie is my wonderful best friend. She's kind of plain Jane—tall, dark hair, and a little clumsy. However, she will fight alongside me for the mentally ill. I love her to pieces! She's the primary secretary for the office and does the day-to-day stuff, but she's not afraid to pull my files and sit in my office to work late, just because. Sometimes it was because we had nothing better to do.

She's the girl who has been there and done that; her husband was a no-good, cheating bastard too. However, she was smarter than I was. She came home one day early; I went with her. She insisted we stop at her house. I was driving when she said, "Let's blow past my house please. I just feel like I need to see something." Of course, the look on her face combined with that nervous energy she was emitting told me that there was more than met the eye. We dropped our heels outside the door and crept in, hearing a whole bunch of shit upstairs. I wanted to stop her from climbing those stairs, but I knew if I stopped her, it wouldn't be the closure she needed to end it. We both climbed those stairs quietly. Hearing her husband with another woman giggling upstairs in their bedroom was beginning to break my heart. I held her hand as it was beginning to sweat. We ended up on the landing on the second floor, and I pulled her back a little. She turned and looked at me with those little brown doe eyes already beginning to cry. I squeezed her hand a little and motioned for us to leave back down the stairs, but she's every bit as strong willed as I am. She shook her head, mouthing the words, "I have to see." I squeezed her hand again, reassuring her that I wasn't going to leave her; I was going to follow this through until the end.

I listened to her sniffle softly, and we were a mere few feet from the door. I'm not sure if I wanted to cry with her or kick both of their asses the second that door opened. We heard them again in the bedroom, reaching climax. Jeannie opened the door, and we both entered quietly. The two of them were so involved with each other that they didn't even see us. I motioned for her to take out her cell and start filming, and she did. She caught the whole thing on video.

Well, the bouncy whore romping all over Jeannie's husband was the neighbor he often insisted to Jeannie she was crazy for worrying about, stating that he and the neighbor were just friends.

The whole divorce did not work out well for him, especially because we had everything on video. There was definitely no "he said, she said," and Jeannie and I have never been closer friends!

I then begin thinking about the time back in my apartment when we got so damn drunk, crying over lost loves and how we had both been broken. We were drinking merlot, having fun, and listening to my iPod. Just then Jeannie heard one of her favorite songs, "Broken" by some little country girl. I knew all the words. As the song began to play, she immediately broke out into song! We were in our pajamas and soon were singing and dancing. We then sat down, hearts beating out of our chests. We started talking about how Tino screwed me over with some psycho whore, saying that she did forensics! Jeannie looked at me and said, "That bitch was nothing but a wannabe! She couldn't put a patch on your ass! Wannabe psych nurse whore!" She turned on "'Girlicious" and "Like Me," and then she pulled me to my feet again, and we danced and sang our hearts out! She said, "Shake that ass, girl! She ain't got shit on you!"

Oh God, that was a good night, snapping out of my throwback of sorts and trying to refocus on work. I have a smile on my face while the whole team gathers around this table to discuss our plans for the day.

I'm sitting in my own little world, giving our clients' baselines and borderlines, stating if someone is critical and needs to be seen by the team and last if not least if I had Courts, when and where. While sitting there surrounded by our community treatment team, I feel that all in all things have been pretty good—up until now.

The team meeting wraps up, and everyone mulls around the office in their own cliques, discussing what went on during the meeting and how everything is supposed to be better. Here I am, completely on cloud nine. I can't wait to get the hell out of here. I take my paperwork with all my writings about all our clients, including their vital information, and walk back into my office. I just want to grab that phone, go into the darkest corner I can, and call him back. While sitting on the heater in front of the window overlooking the city, I take a deep breath and close my eyes for just a moment. I look up at the clouds and then close my eyes again. Oh, I just want to hear his voice. I want to smell him, taste him. I can remember when I first met him.

I was newly separated from Tino and wasn't looking for a relationship, let alone another friend. I was driving to work, and my car engine stalled for no reason. I looked in the rearview mirror and could see the angry faces of other people trying to make it to work like me. Just then, I saw orange and white beacon lights flashing from behind me. I looked, and it was a shiny black tow truck. I thought to myself, *What luck!* He pulled up in front of me, backed up to the front of my car, and motioned for me to come into his truck, so I did. Just then, two metal claws came out from behind the truck and attached themselves to the two front wheels of my crappy little 1992 Toyota Camry. He jumped out of his truck and hopped into my car for a moment, turning my flashers on. Then back into the truck he came.

After he towed my car out of the lanes of traffic, I turned to my savior and said, "Thank you so much! I really thought I was going to be a goner back there!"

He smiled at me and said, "Do you want to take her back to my garage? It's only a few blocks up the road."

I looked over this man who was happy to help me. I nodded and said, "Yes, please."

We drove through the traffic for another five minutes. He said, "Where are you supposed to be?"

I said, "Oh yeah, I have to call work and tell them that I will be late."

The strange and attractive man who came to save my day then said to me, "Let me take this back and try and start it, and I will take you to work. When you are done, call me and I will pick you up—unless of course your husband will mind, and then he can pick you up instead."

I was ever so quick to stop this very good-looking man from making a huge mistake. "No, no. I am not married. Not any more, at least. it's just me. I honestly don't know what happened to my car. It was fine yesterday, when I was at the market. Then I was making a really nice dinner, and then… well, I guess I am up for a terrible week." I tried to stay focused on the car, and not on the fact that my other savior, the one who rescued me from an attacker while I was leaving a client's home, was a no-show for dinner. My ever fleeting thought of my ex was being an idiot, and everything seemed to be falling apart around me. This poor guy just wanted to make some money and not listen to all my drama. I fought the urge to cry huge, sobbing tears and let it all out. I screamed in my head, *Get it together!*

I sighed deeply and put my hands over my face for a moment. I looked over to him, tried to get a grip on my racing thoughts, and smiled slightly at my savior of the day. I wanted to hide the fact that I felt that my whole world was crashing down around me, and I thought that I was turning a corner … when I invited a complete stranger to dinner. There was something comforting, even familiar about him. It took my breath away. I was almost entranced, just staring.

He smiled at me with this gorgeous set of teeth, the kind of smile that is so damned contagious that I had to smile too, or I would die where I stood. I snapped out of it, smiled back at him, and said, "Um, I can call you, and you will pick me up at my job? Are you sure that won't be a problem?"

He turned into the parking lot of his garage, and just as he was about to shift the truck into reverse, he smiled and said, "It would be no problem at all, pretty lady. I will give you my number. You call, and I will come."

I looked into those gorgeous hazel eyes—the most gorgeous eyes I had ever seen! His eyes almost hypnotized me. The brown and gold, living together in that gorgeous face in such harmony. I nodded and muttered, "Okay." I smiled back at him, almost wanting to fall into his aroma of garage grease and dirt, completely lost in this moment.

I am unceremoniously brought back to reality. Jeannie is pinching the back of my arm to get my attention, "Hey, I sure would love to know what is on your mind, to have a grin like that!"

"Sorry, I was just thinking to myself about someone."

"Okay, who is this Mr. Wonderful who has all of your attention during the meeting and has put you on a cloud so high not even I can bring you down?"

Jeannie peers down both long halls of the office and sees that no one is coming. She looks back at me, and I wave for her to come in; she closes the door and sits down. Like two giddy little girls, we sit close to the window in my office so that no one can overhear.

"His name is James, and we met a few months ago. He is the man who rescued me when my car broke down. He is wonderful and everything that I wanted and more."

"What did you do?" Jeannie looked at me with those persecuting eyes, almost knowing that I had something, if not everything, to do with the demise of this relationship.

I feel the intense weight of her stare and quickly balk under her speechless pressure. "I was insecure. I saw him with other women hanging all over him one day, and I guess instead of talking to him about it, I just bowed out gracefully. I didn't want a confrontation like I did with Tino. I just can't have another relationship like that. I didn't want my memory of this relationship with James to be that he had lied to me, that they were 'just friends,' and that I am 'crazy' because there is nothing going on—only to find out later that there really was and I was a complete fool for not trusting my instincts."

"Okay, firstly with Tino, he only said that you were crazy and nuts because he needed to maintain control over you. That is what abusive womanizers do! They use those words as a means to manipulate you so you don't seek help or advice from professionals, or listen to your friends. He was emotionally abusing you. Secondly, I don't know James, but he is a tow truck driver and is with people every day. I would imagine that maybe you let a little baggage from Tino interfere with you and James."

"Yes, maybe I did." The phone rings again.

"Is that James?" she asks.

"Yes."

"Call him back, Charity. Give him a chance. He must really care about you if he keeps calling you."

"Okay, I will call him back."

"We have the rest of the day to do the damn thing!" We laugh together about the job we have, because it is stressful.

"I have the cases, if you want to go over them before you go get them before court, as well as their service plans."

"Okay, sure!"

We go through our client list one by one, mulling through their cases and service plans almost to exhaustion. Soon it's lunchtime.

"Do you want to order in Chinese?" I ask, puckering my lips like a fish.

Jeannie laughs and says. "Yes, but this time no sushi for me. I'm no good with the chopsticks, and I hate soy sauce!"

"Oh, but that is the best part, Jean-Jean! Are you ordering, or am I?"

Jeannie stands up and gathers all the files and service plans for the courts. "I'll make copies of all that you will need for later this afternoon and the itinerary. You order me something fried and bad for me," she instructs, smiling as she walks away.

I pick up the phone and call the Chinese Garden on First Avenue. I put my order in for the sushi box and the fried rice and wonton soup, still perusing the menu. I throw in a Chinese stir fry for Jeannie. It comes to about twenty-five bucks. "Thank you," I say as I hang up the phone. I pick up the phone and start to doodle on my notepad: "J-A-M-E-S." I keep going over the same letters, making them darker and darker until Jeannie comes back in and catches me.

"Whoa! Hey, are you all right?"

"Um, yeah. I called and got you something good but bad for ya, and my sushi box." I turn around in my chair to look at the clock behind me on the window sill, and I see that the time is 11:15 a.m. "Lunch will be here in about fifteen minutes, so we will eat, go over these cases, and get them organized. Then we'll walk to the courthouse and meet everyone there. Hopefully everyone who is supposed to be there will be, and no one will be violated and thrown in the Allegheny County Jail." I look at her as I put both of my hands over my face and then run my fingers through my hair.

We walk our happy little asses up the street with our four cases of the day. We're in tennis shoes but are well dressed besides that. This is the norm in Pittsburgh: always running! Hours pass as I present our clients' cases to the court, exhibiting that they have been complying with all the stipulations of their service plans. This hearing is a mere monthly reporting to let the Mental Health court know each of these clients have gone to their prospective groups, and have complied with probation by paying fines and restitutions or doing community service. Jeannie and I wrap things up, talking to our clients and telling them to keep up the good work. We will talk to them after the long holiday coming up. Some of them are taking holidays with their families, and they deserve it. Many have worked hard toward their sobriety and understanding their mental health; they have taken many a difficult step toward changing their behaviors to better their lives by addressing their mental illnesses.

I stand there for a moment, watching as our clients walk out of the courtroom, laughing and high-fiving each other for a job well done. I sigh, smile, and utter under my breath, "Good job, everyone. Good job indeed!"

Jeannie interrupts the moment with. "Damn! Snow again!"

I turn around in this very old courtroom, and the smell of old wood and marble fills my lungs as much as it fills my heart. I let out a laugh. "Ha! Well what did you want it to do? It is supposed to be cold this time of year, ya know!" I look at her. "Do we have everything together?"

She walks over to the table in the right side of the room, where there is a small stack of files sitting alone. Just a few hours ago there were many stacks of files. "Yes, I think we are," she answers hurriedly as she wraps her scarf around her neck many times until there is barely any face left to see.

I turn to her and laugh. "Jeannie, please. It's not the ice age." I walk over, adjust her scarf, and button her up around her face. I fix her hat so that she will be covered from the rough wind we get downtown. The wind blows right up off the water in downtown Pittsburgh. We have to cover up down here; if not, we will surely get frostbite pretty quickly.

My phone is burning up again. Jeannie looks at me, now peering above her peach scarf. I smile at her. "Yes, yes, it's him. Let's get back to the office, okay?"

We make it to the elevator in the courthouse, each taking four files to carry. We step out of the elevator, and I bundle up just as we walk out. We lock our arms and walk the four blocks to our office, almost racing into our building and trying to stay warm.

"So Jean-Jean, what are you doing for the holidays?"

Jeannie huffs and puffs through her scarf. "Um, I think I am going to go spend time with my parents and see my crazy brothers."

I growl under my breath. "Grr, there's that word."

"Oh, sorry. My partially, not quite mentally ill brothers who like to pick on me because it's their favorite pastime."

"What you're dying to say is your douche bag older brothers will be there to pick on you and pick out every small, insignificant anomaly in your life that you didn't do, in order to make themselves feel better—because you can take care of yourself, and they feel insecure and need a woman to take care of them!"

"Wow, Charity, you summed that up. I'll have to remember all that when they start ragging on me!"

We finally arrive at our building, and we both reach for the door to enter.

"Oh my God, it is cold out there!" I say to her as we both enter the building.

"Who are you telling sister!" she says to me. We both smile and then go to enter the elevator and press the button for the fifth floor. My phone begins to buzz again. Jeannie yanks my arm this time. "You do realize you do have to at least call him, don't you?"

"Yes, yes, I know. Let's just put the notes in the files, make some case notes, and then lock up the files and call it a day."

When we are all done, I say, "Now go home, Jeannie. You have a long drive and a long week ahead of you."

Jeannie puts on her coat and then comes over to hug me. I hug her back. We both look at the clock on the wall and know it is the end of the day. She then puts her scarf around her neck, buttons up her coat, walks over to the door, winks, and heads out.

I am left alone with my thoughts, looking out the window and then at the plaque on my wall of the Pittsburgh Steelers. Then I look outside again at the city of Pittsburgh, City of Champions. I don't feel much like a champion today. What do I do? Should I call him back? Should I go down the garage? Decisions, decisions. I run my fingers through my long blonde hair. "Argh!"

I reach into my desk drawer and pull out a nickel; I see no quarters, but I figure this is good enough. Heads, I call him; tails, I go to the garage.

I flip it up into the air, catch it with my hand, and then slap it on the back side of my left hand. I lift my hand, and it is tails. I take a huge breath. "Damn! I'm such a chump!" I sit in front of my desk and pull out the makeup case I have in my drawer. I take my compact mirror and begin to redo my makeup. I do my eyes and my lips just the way he likes them to be. *Okay, I think I am ready.*

Chapter 2

My heart is pounding out of my chest as I walk to my car. The pavement under my shoes seems to have a heartbeat of its own, beating into my feet. I make it to my car and sit in the driver's seat; the key is in the ignition, and I put my head on the steering wheel. "Oh, God! Please don't let me make a complete fool of myself today. Please." I turn the key and begin to drive. James's garage isn't all that far from work, and as I get closer, my heart pounds harder.

I pull into the garage's lot and park. It is close to the end of his day, so I know there should be close to no one here. I get out of the car, walk into the garage, and over to where James is usually working.

I see him. He is standing underneath a 1999 GMC, fixing what looks like an exhaust pipe. He is dirty—just the way I love him. He has his safety glasses on as he looks down and sees me walking toward him. He quickly stops what he is doing, ducks his head out from under the Jimmy, and walks over to me.

He looks at me, his eyes glazing over, saying no words. He points me to a chair in the corner of the garage. I quickly walk over to the chair and watch as he races across the garage to shut it down. He hits the pad on the wall, and the garage doors come down and lock automatically. He quickly runs past me, locks the front office doors, turns off the lights and computers, and shuts and locks the door behind him. He takes a deep breath while standing in front of me. He then leans down, holding on to the armrests of the chair, leaning into me. Sweat runs down the sides of his face.

He says calmly and with restraint in his voice, "Where have you been? Why haven't I seen you? Why haven't you taken my calls?"

I go to open my mouth, but I look up at him and see the hurt in his eyes, the frustration that I had to have caused him, and the worry that he must have felt. My own eyes fill with tears. "I saw you with those…"

Just as I go to complete my sentence, James grabs me around my waist, pulling me into him hard. The tears stream down my face as he kisses me deep. His tongue invades my mouth and wraps itself around my soul. It is as though I have died, and he breathes his life into me, pouring his soul into mine. I have felt empty and alone, but no longer. He runs his hands all over my body. He lifts my skirt and tears off my clothes. Tears stream down my face as I wonder how I could have been so stupid. He takes off his overalls and every piece of clothing, demanding my body be wrapped around his. He pulls me onto him. "Come here, baby."

I sigh deeply as he pulls my body onto his long thick shaft. *Oh my God!* His lips are all over my mouth, my breasts, my nipples, and my neck. He bites my neck ever so softly, reminding me that I am his, all his. I begin to hold my breath, not wanting to have this moment escape me. He pulls my head back, licking my neck and running his teeth down my neck. "Baby, breathe. Breathe, baby."

I sigh, running my nails down his back as his back arches, thrusting his girth deep into my body. "Oh my God!"

We move together rhythmically as our bodies become one. He is deeper and deeper into my soul with every thrust. My body lusts for him. My heart yearns for his love. My soul lives only for him. He slows down a moment and looks at me. "Please don't run from me again, baby. I love you. I need you. You're my best friend, my lover, my everything. I need you."

I look up at this man who is so strong and loving. "I love you, James."

He smiles down at me, and then he leans down and kisses me like his life depends on it, deeply and warmly and with so much love it even made God pause. He begins to thrust into me hard and long, grabbing my breasts and touching every part of me. There isn't one inch of my being that escapes his touch.

We make love all night long. and as we do, he claims me—my mind, my body, and even my soul—with growing intensity.

It is nearly four in the morning, and we are both extremely exhausted. James stands up, and I see his gorgeous body, tattoos and all. He walks toward his office desk and attempts to grab his underwear and socks. I watch him for a few moments as he puts on his socks. I look carefully at the cross tattoo on his back. It is beautiful and sits perfectly on his right shoulder. As it comes down, it almost hooks slightly to the right. The edges are beveled, and along the edges are either a design or some strange, um, something.

I say, "Baby, can I see that for a moment, please?"

"See what, baby?" he says as he turns his head slightly to acknowledge my question.

"Your tattoo on your back. I just want a closer look at it. What does it mean?"

He smiles as he leaps up with his pants now completely on, redirecting me, "Let's go home, baby."

I nod with extreme exhaustion, and he wraps me up in a shop blanket, puts me into the front of his car, and closes the door. He puts his coveralls back on and grabs his keys. I am lying but sitting in the front seat, awaiting his arrival. He comes into to the car, shuts the door, leans over to me, and kisses me. "That's my baby." He clicks the garage door open as we pull out and are on our way.

I smile to myself as I lay there wrapped up in this blanket. We drive to his house, he clicks the garage door open, and we pull in. The garage door closes. I must have nodded off along the way because I wake up to him pulling me out of the car and carrying me inside. "Oh honey, I can walk," I say.

"No, baby, I've got you."

James gently lays me down on the bed. He had the electric blanket on, and the bed is nice and warm. He pulls the shop blanket off of me, and I let out a bit of a whine. James says, "Baby, I will be there in a minute to help keep you warm." I lie there in his bed, smelling him again, tasting him, feeling him all over me again. I know now that this is exactly where I want to be, right here with him.

James slides his naked body up against mine. "Come here, baby. Put your body up against mine." I turn around and press my body completely up against his, knowing that his heat will keep me warm and his aroma will lull me to sound slumber.

I awaken to James many hours later between my legs, tasting me. He reaches up, pinches my nipples softly, and then slides two fingers deeply inside of me. After climbing on top of my body, he kisses me softly while he uses those fingers to lift my pelvis up and down deep inside. He flicks my clit with his thumb and is lifting with more force now. I feel like I am going to pee myself, and I tell him so. He smiles and says, "Do it." It's because he knows that's not what it is. He wants me to come, and I want to make him happy, so I calm down and breathe. Just when I think I am going to pee, I let it go.

"Oh. My. God!" I scream so loudly that God can hear me! My whole body trembles as I make James very wet, and he is loving it! He doesn't stop thrusting those fingers into me, making me do it again. Now my whole body is trembling. He is so hard and erect now, and I am so sensitive.

James mounts me as he spreads my legs wide, lifting my legs, bending my knees, and pushing them down and holding them by the ankles. He slides his cock deep inside of my wet pussy. I am so warm, wet, and sensitive that I feel like I am going to cum any minute. He is pounding my pussy hard like he owns it. He slides his thumb down and rubs my clit as he pounds my pussy with his cock. He reaches down, grabs my nipples, and pinches them hard. It hurts me, but he is so turned on by that—and admittedly, so am I. He thrusts his cock into my pussy hard and long, filling me until my pussy can't hold any more of his love juices.

He lays next to me, his chest rising and falling rapidly, and then it slows to a more relaxed state. He wraps me up into his arms, and as I lay there, it occurs to me: that one fleeting thought. It's the thought that strikes fear in the hearts of men and warriors from around the globe. James notices a change in my body language. He pulls me away from him to look at me and says, "What's the matter, baby?"

I start to quietly sob. "You won't love me anymore if I tell you."

He holds me closer to him. "Don't be silly. What's on your mind?"

"After I stopped coming around, I stopped taking anything for birth control."

"Baby, I don't care. I love you. You belong to me. You are mine! I want you to be the mother of our children—just you, only you! Come here, my baby, and let's get some sleep."

I listen to James tell me he loves me, wants me. He wants me to be the mother of his children! Could he be what I have been waiting for my whole life? Can he be the one to breathe the life back into me? I curl up into him, feeling his warmth and the warmth of the blanket and bed. For once I feel safe and secure.

For this fleeting moment, I toy with the idea. What would life be like? Could there finally be a "happily ever after" for me, for us? I know we are both so very damaged. I finally close my eyes, knowing that yes, we are damaged, but he is *my* damaged baby, and I am his. I snuggle a little closer, deeper into his arms, protected by his love.

Chapter 3

I feel the sun on my face, and I open my eyes to see James wrapped around me. The sun glistens off of his brown hair, highlighting his perfect jaw line, his gorgeous goatee, and the sexy beauty mark on his cheek. Oh, how I love to stare upon him dreamily. I lean in to kiss this gorgeous man I love, and he smiles at me with his eyes closed and pulls me into him with both arms, squeezing while he buries his face into my neck, kissing me and beating me to the punch. He rolls me on top of him. I kiss him softly and deeply, moving my long blonde hair to one side so that I don't get my hair in his face. He pulls it back so that he can stare at me a long minute. He sighs and says, "God, you are so beautiful."

I feel like I want to cry because no one has ever said that to me, let alone made me feel that way before. I lean down and kiss him as though he means the world to me. I look at him and smile awkwardly, sitting above him.

James smiles up at me. "What is that look for, beautiful?"

I am straddling him with my hands clasping his above his head, moving my hips in a swaying, grinding motion and being a little mischievous. I look down at him, kiss him slowly, and whisper, "Baby, someone ripped all my clothes off last night in the heat of passion, so I guess I have to be nakey all day long." I use a cute, coy voice, smiling.

James grins ear to ear, "Well, maybe my master plan was to keep you naked and to have my way with you, so that I can have you whenever I want."

I smile at him and know in my heart and soul that there isn't anything I wouldn't do for him, including parading around in my birthday suit.

He kisses me, slides me to the right side of him on the bed, and gets up and walks to his dresser. I gaze at the way the sun catches his silhouette. His body isn't perfect; he has some scars from his time in the military and a little belly. But he is still mine. I still love looking at his tattoos on his arms and on his back. He looks back at me staring at him, smiling and licking my lips. He reaches into a drawer and grabs a V-neck T-shirt and a pair of boxer briefs. He puts on the pair of boxer briefs. He then walks over, sits on the bed, slowly strokes my face, and kisses me. He hands me the shirt and says, "Here, my beautiful baby, this will make you a little more comfortable while I make you something to eat." He leans in to kiss me again and then walks down the hall, humming to himself happily.

While lying in the bed where we had made love all night, I have a momentary daydream. I wonder, *Is this real?*

He yells up to me in the bedroom. "Hey sleepy, are you coming down for breakfast? I made coffee."

I smile to myself. "Yeah, on my way!" I run down the stairs to the kitchen, and he has breakfast almost finished. I sit down at the table, in awe of him. He puts the buttered toast and the eggs, sunny side up, on my plate. He turns to me to put my plate on the table, but he stops and says, "I remember you love your eggs sunny side up, and two pieces of rye, extra butter." He sets the plate in front of me, and I look up at him so happy that I choke back tears. "What's the matter, baby?"

"You remembered. You remembered how I take my eggs, and how I love extra butter on my toast."

"Of course I do! I love you! Oh, here, I made your coffee. a little coffee with your cream and sugar beautiful." I get up and hug him hard. He hugs me back. "I know everything about you because I want to know everything about you. You mean the world to me."

I sit across from him in awe, smiling, and we eat our breakfast together.

"I have to go back down to the garage today so that I can finish a couple of things to get them out of there and put some money in our pockets," he says, smiling and shoveling the last bit of his breakfast in his mouth.

Feeling like I am being pushed out the door, and I quickly think I need to save face. I put my guard up, thinking that I have made an epic mistake. Choking back my heart and everything I was feeling last night, I clear my throat, look down at my coffee, and say, "Oh, okay. Um." I am almost choked up, thinking last night was not what I thought or hoped it was. "I guess I should go home, then." I make sure that he doesn't see me about to cry. I sip my coffee slowly, hiding part of my face and looking away.

He looks at me, perplexed, and then he detects that my entire body language has changed and that I can't lookay up from my cup. He says with hope in his voice, "I thought you were home, baby, but if you want to go back to your place and start bringing your things back home, *here* where you belong, that would be great."

Sitting there hiding my face from him, he carefully puts my cup down and helps me to stand up. He then picks me up to sit on his lap, moving my wavy hair away from my face to reveal those tears quietly streaming down my face. After looking deeply into my eyes, he kisses me, slow and beautiful. We stop kissing, and he lifts up my chin to look at him.

"You're even beautiful when you're in tears for no reason at all." He gently wipes them from my face. "Honey, I love you and can't live without you. I have so many things I want to share with you, do with you—no one else, just you. So please, go back to your place and bring your things home. Please?" He kisses my nose and smiles at me with those gorgeous eyes and beautiful teeth.

I can never tell this man no. I nod as the tears stream down my face. Then I clear my throat slightly. "Yes, honey, I will pack everything up and come home." He hugs me so tightly that I feel like I will break. I close my eyes and breathe him in deeply.

He laughs, saying, "Oh, I could smell your beautiful scent all day!" After picking me up from the sitting position, he kisses me one quick time and puts me on my feet. "Mmm, sexy! I think I should keep you in that T-shirt every day. Or maybe I should have you walk around here naked for me."

"I would do anything for you, James. Anything to make you happy." I look up into his eyes while we still embrace.

He whispers to me, "Come home. Let me love you. You belong to me." He kisses my forehead. "Now, let's get you some clothes to put on to go over there."

We climb the stairs to our bedroom, and James ruffles through all his clothes. He hands me a pair of his sweatpants and a warm sweatshirt.

As I get dressed, we agree that he is going to drive me to my house so that I can pack and be back in about an hour. We will make plans to pick up the rest later tonight.

We get into the car, and James drives me to my house. He parks the car and leans in to kiss me. "Okay, I will be finished down the garage in an hour, so I hope to see you home."

"Yes, I will have my clothes packed up, and I will be home ASAP."

He reaches for the back of my head and pulls my lips to his. He kisses me so deeply that my heart begins to flutter, and he steals my breath away. I pull back slowly, saying, "I am never going to get home if we don't do what we need to do!" I smile and reach for the door. He winks at me as he looks into his side mirror. I open the door and step out. I close the door and see him staring at me. I wave at him and walk up the stairs to my house. He pulls away as I open the door. I step inside, close the door, and lean up against it for a moment. I sigh and say to myself, "Okay, here we go."

While walking around the house, I gather up my iPod and cord sitting by my laptop on the living room table. I put my laptop into its bag, along with the rest of my work papers. I put my iPod in one of the pockets. Then I go into my bedroom and into my closet. I pull out my blue suitcases and begin loading them with my panties, bras, clothing, and jewelry. I take my smaller bag into the bathroom and pack my toothbrush, toothpaste, shampoo and conditioner, razors, and anything else I can fit in there. Altogether, I load two full suitcases and my small carry bag. I am excited and nervous.

I sit in my living room, where I have been alone for such a long time. I close my eyes and lay my head back on my chair. A million thoughts rush into my mind all at once. I keep thinking about the day I walked in on James with those women so close to his body, challenging him to make a move, to take them like he has taken me so many times. Trusting him wholly and fully is paramount; I can't live like I did in my marriage. I am sickened by the potential thoughts of who is he with, what is he doing, and why. Reflecting on how anxious Tino made me constantly worrying about where he was. Just when I thought that I could trust him, he burned me when I found out he was at a bar, or with that whore nurse up at her house playing house.

I lift my hands up to my head and run my fingers through my hair. Anxiety, frustration, and hurt rush through me once again. I want to trust James. He is not my ex husband. A flood of memories come back to me like a rain storm, needling my heart and mind. No matter how hard I tried, how pretty I tried to be, how smart I was, I was never going to be enough for Tino, nor was I ever going to be good enough for him. He had to be needed and wanted by other women. He had to be their hero, not mine. When I needed him desperately, he wasn't there. He was there for his little nurse, though.

I remember our last few arguments, near the end. I asked Tino. "Where were you when I needed you? Why were you there for her?"

His reply was, "I only talked to the girl but once a month. Did I talk to you once a month?" The difference? He was with her and wasn't with me. I was hospitalized after my head-on collision, He continued to redirect the question. "Well? Did I talk to you more than once a month?"

I knew that I had already lost this fight, as well as my marriage. With tears in my eyes, I nodded.

He said triumphantly, "Well, there ya go!"

I can remember this day as though it were yesterday: the ache it left in my heart, And how it could have marked my very soul. It's amazing how people can be married, and yet one person has it all because he has control. He took control, stole every aspect of my life. He decided how money was spent, and if and when we had sex. He decided if we could have friends over, and he usually made my friends feel unwelcome. Essentially, I was trapped, cornered, and Lonely, feeling lost and contemplating things I would have never entertained otherwise.

As for him? Well, he could give a shit. He wished that I would disappear.

I sit there with my head back, chanting to myself, "Okay, okay, settle down already, breathe! This is a new beginning with someone who desires me, loves me, wants me, devours my lips and takes my breath away! Not someone who I had to beg and plead with to touch me, or have to explain why I needed a hug when I so desperately needed one. He doesn't lie straight to my face or start an argument to tell me, 'this is why I hates you', or the worst yet, the one that cut me to my soul.

Tino had said if he and that whore were loving each other twenty years ago, there never would have been a Charity and Tino. I remember how he said those things to me. The fact that he said that last one thing pierced my love-starved heart executing me with a few brutal words. It was right before Christmas, and I pictured him screaming that at me. I remember the ache in my heart and the agony I withstood that year before I finally left. I sigh deeply, feeling the warmth of the tears stream down my face. I tilt my head forward and wipe them away as I look at the suitcases in front of me. Yup, this is the cleansing I guess I needed, so that I can move forward. I am going to leave all my hurt, frustrations, and insecurities right here!

I get to my feet and put on some of my clothes. I walk out of my bedroom and down the hall to where my coat hangs on a hook. I put it on, lift my hair out over it, and button it up. While walking back into the living room, I have a sigh of relief as I lift the handle out of the suitcases and put the other bag over my shoulder. "Good-bye, painful memories. Good-bye, Tino," I mutter to myself as I reach for the door to leave.

I walk out into the crisp, cold December air, and the sunlight hits me almost immediately. *Thank you, God*, I think to myself as I close the door behind me and walk down my stairs to my older car. I look at this rust bucket that was always breaking down on me all the time. I wonder if it will it start right up, or will this whole thing come full circle, and James will have to come and tow it one more time? Oh how I wish I had my new car here. All this worry would be avoided.

I load my car with my suitcases and then get in. I hold my breath for a moment and turn the key. The engine turns over. *Whew!*

I make it half way down the street when my cell phone rings. I quickly reach into my coat pocket, looking for my Bluetooth. I place the speaker in my ear and arrange the ear hook. By this time the ringing has stopped. I reach for my phone and look for my missed call: it's James. Just as I try to call him back, it rings again, he is calling. A smile comes over my face. *Great minds think alike.* I hit the button to talk and put my phone back into my pocket.

"Hello?"

"Where's my sexy, gorgeous baby? I was just making sure that car of yours started."

"Yes, it did. I am on my way, honey! I should be there in ten," I say. My smile is bigger than ever.

"I can almost hear your smiling! I have a whole day planned for us!"

"You do? What are we going to do?"

"It's a surprise! I want our first day together to be as beautiful as our first night was! I love you!"

"I love you too! I will see you in eight minutes."

"Okay, be careful—you're carrying precious cargo! Bye."

I quickly hang up and then call Jeannie. The phone rings several times, and I start to grow impatient. Finally she says, "Hello?"

"Jean-Jean!"

"Merry merry chickie!"

"Love you!"

"Uh oh! What's going on?" she asks.

"I'm moving in with him."

"What? I know you love him, but a few days ago you couldn't pick up the phone, and now you're moving in?"

"So not like me, huh?"

"Not at all! When are you doing this drastic event?"

"Today."

"Charity!"

I grinned. "I know, I know."

"Look, I love you, and I will stand by you no matter what decision you make. I know you love him too. I also know that you're intelligent and will make good decisions."

"I knew that you'd understand. So, how is your visit going?"

"Oh." She sighs heavily. "Don't ask." Suddenly there is a loud bang in the background, and someone yells. "Honey, I have to go. Call me later tonight if you can, okay? Bye." She suddenly hangs up the phone, I smile, thinking about how chaotic it always is for her when she visits family over the holidays.

I begin to think about James's last words: a surprise. Tino never surprised me with anything; it was always, "You pick the movie," and when I did, he bitched about how stupid it was. During the movie in the theater, he would say under his breath, "Is this over? I'm bored." The most embarrassing thing he ever did to me was when we were in the theater and, the movie was over, he stood up almost immediately and said, "Well, that was two hours I will never get back again!" He pushed his way through the crowd of people exiting, saying, "Smoker! Smoker here! Out of my way!" I remember how people used to lookay at him—and at me running after him, trying to keep up and apologizing as I followed him.

I am anxious to get to James, but I am even more anxious to stop thinking or reminiscing about Tino! I growl as I sit at the red traffic light. I turn on the radio to drown all those thoughts from my mind and my heart. Sia is singing; she has such a powerful, beautiful angelic voice! "Chandelier" is on, and I love this song! I look up, and the light is finally green. Listening to this song takes my mind off of the traffic, Tino, and the length of time it takes to get to my true love.

I turn up the street to James's house. I am halfway down the street and see him standing outside, waiting for me! I speed up a little bit. *God, thank you! Thank you for bringing him back into my life!*

I pull into his driveway slowly, and he runs over to my car as I put it in park. He quickly reaches for my door and helps me unbuckle my seat belt, kissing me while he does. I touch his face as I kiss him back.

"Come on, baby, let's get inside." He opens the back door where I threw the suitcases, pulling them out to take them inside. I shut the back door and go around to the passenger side door to grab my laptop bag, putting the strap over my shoulder to carry it inside. James pulls the two suitcases behind him. The door to the house is unlocked, as we both walk in from the cold. He shuts the door and immediately takes the suitcases up to the bedroom—our bedroom. I walk up behind him. He puts them on the bed, unzips them, and begins putting my clothes away. I smile again, taking my bag off of my shoulder and unbuttoning my coat.

"Okay, so what are we going to do? How should I dress?" I say as I walk over to him, getting close enough to reach for his body. He turns away from the dresser and reaches for me, pulling me into his body, which is now sweaty. I look deep into his gorgeous eyes. His heart is pounding, and his lips are full. I go in for the kiss, and he hugs me.

He holds my head with his hand close to his heart. "Do you hear that?" he asks.

"I hear your heart pounding," I say, smiling to myself.

"Yes! My heart didn't have the life it has now when you left me." He pulls me back from him to look at me. "I love you, I need you! When you left, I was miserable. Please don't leave me again." He looks at me, almost questioning my motives for being back.

"Never, ever again. I don't want to be lonely, hurt, or abandoned again. I know that you love me. I know that." I stop to choke back tears. "I know that you will hug me and not ask why I need a hug. You love me with your soul, not just your body. You're the best friend I have ever had. And most of all…" I am choking on my tears. "Most of all, I can't picture you ever telling me that you hate me!"

"Oh baby!" He pulls me back into his chest. "I want us to always talk, share, love one another. I don't want there to be any secrets between us. I want to marry you and make you mine!" He finishes with almost a guttural growl in his chest.

I say, "I am yours. I belong to you, only you."

He grasp on my back and head loosen, and his breathing gets slower. He pulls me back, saying, "Let's finish getting this stuff put away so that we can get a shower and get outta here!" He releases our embrace and quickly goes back to putting the clothes away. I grab my shower tote and walk into the bathroom to put my things in beside his. I walk toward the shower and look into the mirror. I see a glimpse of a ... tail? Swinging? I quickly turn and see James zipping up the suitcase on the bed.

He looks at me from the end of the bed. "What's wrong, honey?"

"Nothing. Um, I thought I saw something. It was nothing." I smile and turn back to the shower, putting my shampoo and conditioner in the shower stall. I walk back into the bedroom and begin to strip my clothes off to lure him into the shower.

He sits on the bed, staring at the show I am giving him. His eyes are all over my body, and he is growing excited. I take off my ankle socks and make a grand exit as I lift the sock above my head, smiling at him and dropping it on the floor. I slowly turn, walk toward the bathroom, look back, and blow him a kiss. He begins stripping like a crazy person. I run into the bathroom quickly, giggling as I go.

He chases after me barely having his legs out of his jeans. Quickly I turn the water on to straight hot. When I get the water turned on, James is right behind me, pulling me into him. Our naked bodies are together, and I feel his hard cock pressed up against my back as he holds me. I turn around so that I can feel him up against my breasts. His throbbing girth is pressing against my stomach. I kiss him, leading him into the shower with me. The water is hot, just the way we like it. He is kissing me hard as the water bounces off our bodies. I look at him while his hands roam all over my body.

"I love you!" I say before my mouth is invaded by his roaming, ravenous tongue.

He stops for a moment, holding my face with both of his hands. "I love you so much! I would give everything for you!" He smiles at me, and I touch his lips with my finger gently as he takes my face and pulls me into him. He lifts me up, and I wrap my legs around his waist. He leans me up against the back wall of the shower, thrusting his hard cock deep inside of my throbbing, wet pussy. He pounds into me, and I scream in pleasure as his hands go all over my body, muffling my screams of pleasure with his ravenous mouth. I am about to explode with pleasure as his breathing changes. He is grunting and growling in my ear now. I can feel him about to explode deep inside of me. I feel his mouth latch on to my shoulder as he explodes into me with such force that I feel his teeth pierce my skin. He has just bitten me. Within this moment, I loved him biting me and don't know why. He is still inside of me, thrusting his full load into me, still biting me in the same spot. I cum again all over his cock. He unlatches from my shoulder and holds me close to him. While keeping me up against the back wall, he leans back slowly, letting my legs slide down his hips to the floor of the shower. He is panting and holding me; he looks exhausted. I move my head side to side as my neck is starting to thump with pain. I slowly push him back into the water, smiling. "You do that every time we make love!" James looks back at me with this huge smile on his face. His smile lights a fire in my heart.

I turn around to wash my back and I hear him gasp. I turn and ask him, "What's wrong?"

He looks at me horrified. "Oh my God honey, are you okay?"

I smile and say, "I love you!" I dismiss what I know must be bad. But I love him. I finish washing off, and he watches the steams of water mix with my blood running in two direct streams down my back. I step out of the shower to dry off as he steps out behind me, immediately grabbing his red towel to dry me off. I lean over, and almost immediately I am dizzy and about fall over. James catches me around my waist with the towel.

"Whoa! Wow, sorry, baby. Maybe the water was too hot," I say to him, smiling weakly.

He picks me up and carries me to the bed. staring at me as he takes me into the bedroom. His body is still very wet. He lies me on the bed and climbs in next to me. "Honey, do you think you are all right?" he says, choking back tears.

"Worried?" I say as I climb on top of his body, straddling his now semi-erect cock. He puts his hands on either side of my hips. I lean down and kiss him. The dizziness leaves as quickly as it came. I lift back off of his gorgeous face and say, "I am fine, baby! Let's get dressed." I slowly grind into his erection and then seductively dismount his beautiful body, leaving him with thoughts that I always want more of him. which I always will.

After he realizes that I am okay and am getting dressed, he rises from the bed, dries off, and gets dressed as well. I glance over as I see him pulling out his suit. "Honey, I don't really have anything that nice."

"Wear your blue dress. I love that dress," he says, smiling at me while he puts on his dress slacks.

I dry my hair, put on my makeup, and tie up my hair. I slide on my dress and walk out for him to zip up my back.

"Absolutely gorgeous!" he whispers in my neck as he zips me up. He kisses my neck and hugs me from behind as we gaze into the mirror for a moment. I look at us together in the mirror, a couple hugging and completely loving each other. This what I have always wanted—no, what I desperately needed.

"Okay, gorgeous, let's go!" We descend down the stairs. James pulls this long black bag out of the hallway closet. He hangs it up and unzips it. "I know it's going to be very cold tonight, and I don't want my baby cold, so I went and did a little shopping today while you were packing. I bought you this." He turns to me as I stand on the last step in awe. I step down and walk toward this huge bag, almost knowing what it is. I put my hands in it; it's soft and furry, and so I open the bag more. He pulls it out and helps me put it on. I squeak a little and bounce. He lets out a laugh as he pulls out this gorgeous long black fur coat and places it around me. It's warm and beautiful! It goes down to my ankles.

I hug him, almost jumping on him. I kiss him so deeply that it feels as though I am taking his breath away.

"Do you know how much I love you?" he says. I look into his eyes with tears slowly filling my own. I nod without words, confirming his love for me. James laughs lightly and says as he gets his coat on, "You're about to find out!"

We walk down the basement stairs and into the garage.

I can't speak at this moment. I am slowly taking it all in as he opens his car door for me. I slide in, and he covers me up with my beautiful coat before closing the door. He races around the car and gets in.

We drive downtown. He pulls into the Grand Gatherer parking lot and heads to the valet. He opens the door as the valet takes his keys, and another valet opens my door. The man reaches for my hand but is quickly interrupted by James saying, "I've got this. Thanks." James gently takes my hand and helps me out of the car. He places my arm around his as he leads me into the restaurant.

I am in awe as I am led by the man I love into the most beautiful place I have ever seen. I can smell the antique wood around me, and it is all so beautiful. There are many beautiful tables with candles on them. James and I walk up to the lady greeting people, and James gives his name. "James Angel." That name is beautiful, and I think, *I can't wait to meet his parents.*

The waiter comes and tells James that our table is ready. He guides us to a beautiful table by the window overlooking the river. He pours us champagne and hands us a menu. He then tells us the specials, and James orders for me. I smile, looking across the table at this beautiful, thoughtful man. My eyes are so amazed by the scenery. This has to be the most beautiful restaurant I have ever been in. The woodwork was done when men took pride in their work.

James reaches for my hand across the table. "Do you like this, baby?"

"Oh my God, yes! I love it!," I say in a whisper. "It's beautiful!"

"Good, I am glad you like it. I want tonight to be as beautiful and memorable, forever," he says as he reaches for his champagne glass. He takes a small sip and asks, "How is your neck? Honey, I am so sorry I got carried away. I always seem to lose myself with you."

I smile as I stare at him with the beautiful glow of candlelight. "I love you with all of my heart, James. I love you! I am fine—in fact, I am more than fine! You know, I am starting to think that you didn't go to the garage at all, and that you went out to buy this gorgeous coat for me, and to plan this beautiful dinner in this gorgeous restaurant. All for me." I squeeze his hand and lean over to kiss him.

He moves his seat closer to mine and leans in to kiss me, slowly touching my face as he molds his mouth to mine. He kisses me slowly and deeply, stealing my breath away as we breathe together as his lips wrap gently over mine. Our moment is interrupted by the waiter bringing our salad hearts.

The waiter places each plate down in front of us. I look up and ask for dressing, as he brings a tiny pour pitcher with ranch dressing. "Oh, thank you," I say as he walks away from our table.

"Honey, I have something I want to ask you," James says as his voice begins to crack a little. He rises from his seat, pulling something from his coat pocket, and takes one knee in front of me. "I love you, Charity Colette Henry. You're no one's consolation prize. You are the prize. Will you marry me and make me the happiest man on Earth?" His eyes are tearing up, and his hand is shaking a little. He looks almost nervous as he asks me this one very important question.

I am bouncing and vibrating with excitement in my seat, as there are tears streaming down the back of my eyes. "Yes! James, yes! I will be your wife!"

You know that moment when you hold your breath. and all you see is him? Your ears ring a little, time almost stops, and you want it to. You stop breathing, and then ...

James places the most gorgeous ring on my finger, picks me up from my seat, and kisses and hugs me. I can't hear anyone clapping and whistling in the background at first, until he sets me back on my feet. Usually, I see only him. I breathe for him, live for him; everything else is just background.

The waiter waits until the applause and whistling dies down to bring our meals. "Congratulations to the both of you! On behalf of the Grand Gathering, tonight's entire meal is on us. Enjoy!"

James shakes his hand and says, "Thank you very much. We appreciate that!"

The waiter leaves the table, and I am staring down at the most gorgeous piece of jewelry that I have ever seen. It is a one carat, marquis-cut diamond solitaire. "Oh honey ..." I look into his eyes. "This is gorgeous. This whole night is wonderful!"

"Now you are mine, all mine, my gorgeous. My sexy, soon-to-be wife!" He begins to eat his dinner, smiling at me in between forkfuls of food.

We finish our meal by drinking the champagne. James only drinks part of his champagne as he is driving us home soon.

After we finish our meal and get up to grab our coats, the waiter comes to the table with a manila envelope. "Here is the information you requested, sir, about our wedding packages." My jaw drops as James finishes putting my coat on me and thanks the waiter for bringing the information in such a timely manner.

"Let's go home, gorgeous." He pushes in my chair and takes my arm in his.

All the staff we pass on our way out the door, as well as many customers, congratulate us on our engagement. I am smiling bigger than I ever thought possible. My heart is so full of joy that I don't know what to do.

We walk outside, and the valet brings us James's car and gives James a handshake, congratulating him. James opens the door for me, and I sit. The door closes, and the next thing I know, James and I are driving home.

"Honey, are you really okay? Or are you just in shock?" he said, smiling over at me while also paying attention to the road.

"Oh my God! This is such a beautiful ring! And the whole night was … beautiful and wonderful! I can't wait for us to get home!" I don't realize that my voice is getting loud with my excitement, but he doesn't complain. He is elated, and I am so excited.

We pull into the garage to the house and walk down the hall of the basement to the stairs. I take my shoes off, sliding them off of my foot while holding on to the banister to the stairs. James is standing right there with me, loving me with his eyes. I stand on the first step, turn, and look him in the eyes. "James Angel, I can't wait to be your wife and the mother of our children. Many, many children!"

He doesn't wait for any further reaction from me. He pulls me into his strong body, wrapping his arms around my back with one hand on the back of my head, kissing me with all his breath. "You belong to me, only me, just me. You're mine now."

I look into his eyes. He is different, Strong, affirming. "Yes, my husband. I belong only to you."

He turns me slowly to walk up the stairs. "The night is not over yet."

I am excited as I race up the stairs to the first floor and then head straight to our bedroom. I take off my gorgeous coat and hang it up on a hanger in our closet. He has his jacket and his tie off, and he is unbuttoning his shirt as he walks toward me. He rips his shirt off and throws it on the chair in the corner of the room. He unzips and drops his pants to the floor. I watch as his undressing is like a dance, his steps carefully placed as he comes towards me from across the room, until he is standing naked, fully erect and larger than I have ever seen him before. He pulls me hard toward him, turns me around, unzips my dress, and unsnaps my bra. He reaches for my breasts from the back. "Ahh," I sigh deeply as he licks my neck where he bit me earlier, and he slowly strips off my clothes.

I can feel his heart beating through his fingertips as he reaches down and rips my panties into pieces. I am so turned on by this that I don't even care. He picks me up and lays me on the bed, spreading my legs as he falls to the edge onto his knees. He pulls my wet, thumping pussy to his mouth and buries his tongue deep inside of me. I arch up in pleasure as he becomes more forceful with me. His sucking on my clit and burying his tongue deep inside me is bringing me quickly to climax. "I'm cumming. May I cum, please?" I say with desperation.

He penetrates my pussy deeper with is tongue. "Yes! Cum now!" He pulls me closer into his ravenous mouth. I cum and my body shakes, and I scream.

He refuses to let me go. I can't take the stimulation of him down there anymore. I try to push him away, but he smacks both of my hands away and grabs them instantly and holds them as he continues to fuck me with his glorious tongue. He sucks on my clit and buries his tongue deep inside of me. *My God, I am such a lucky woman!* I can feel my body tensing up again, and he is ravaging my very wet pussy with his mouth. He is growling and licking and flicking his tongue on and off of my throbbing clit. I am cumming again.

"May I cum, please?" I say, my voice tired from all the screaming in pleasure he is subjecting my body to. He doesn't answer but continues to lick in that spot. I am arching because it feels as though I am going to pee right there on the bed. Horrified, I scream at him to stop. but he keeps doing it. I break a sweat, my heart is pounding, and then it releases. I scream with each thrust of this new feeling. "Oh my God! Oh my God!" I squirt out a liquid all over his face and his chest.

"Now *that's* how I want you to cum for me, everyday!" Wiping his face as he climbs on top, he slides his immense girth deep inside of me. He feels thicker and longer than I remember. He grasps my breasts hard, using them as leverage while he pounds my pussy hard. He can feel me get tighter and tighter as he knows I am about to cum. "Cum for me. Cum on my dick!"

I look at the intent in his eyes and let go. I don't know how much longer I can keep this up; I have never felt like this before. He holds my hands in one hand above my head and pinches my nipples hard with the other hand. I scream in pain and pleasure as he thrusts harder into my body with his thick, hard cock. I feel pain mixed with pleasure; my body feels confused. My heart pounds for more of him. I beg him, "Fuck me! Fuck me harder! Claim me!"

He is pounding as hard and as fast as he possibly can. "Argh!" He looks into my eyes, and his eyes are different. Fear takes over. I lean up to kiss him. He grabs me by my throat and slams me back down onto the bed as he still cums hard inside of me. He loosens his grip on my throat and collapses on top of my body. I run my fingers through his sweaty hair and down his back with my nails. He's exhausted, and he slowly dismounts from my creamy white thighs and lies next to me. "Come here, baby," he says.

I roll toward him on the bed, and he takes my hand, staring at my hand with the ring he just put on hours earlier.

"I thought you would love this. I looked through droves of engagement rings, and this one spoke to me."

I am so tired that I hear almost all of that before I stretched over to kiss his lips, but I soon collapse into sleep.

It's late Sunday morning. James quietly descends downstairs in order to not wake me. After walking into the kitchen, he begins to make coffee. He pulls the container out from under the counter and fills up the pitcher full of water. He walks back over to the counter and puts the coffee pot together to brew.

"Congratulations, son!"

"Dad!"

"I think you should have given me a heads-up as to what you were planning on doing, don't you think?"

"No, I don't. I got her back, and I am not going to lose her again. To no one!"

"Why this girl? Why does it have to be *this* girl?"

James peers at his father, who is dressed in a black suit. He has dark hair, brown and green eyes, and no facial hair. "Do I have to explain it to you, Father? I love her. I want her—forever!" He is getting steadily irritated with his father's sudden intrusion into his home.

"You want her? She isn't like us, so how do you think she is going to react? To you or to us for that matter." His father walks closer to James.

"She loves me. She gives herself to me wholly. I do not have any worry that she won't accept me. I have every intention of marrying her. She will have all of my children, and it will only be her!" James is increasingly aggravated about this line of questioning, and he slams the coffee cup on the counter.

"Son, try to understand … I know you already bit her. How are you going to handle your urges and not kill her?" Now his father sits at the counter, concerned.

"Dad, she will do what is necessary to please me. She calms me and brings out the best in me. When I touch her, I feel as though I belong. It's meant to be. I will kill someone to protect her, as well as our future together. That is how I feel, Father." He looks at his father with something he hasn't seen in at least one hundred years: humanity and a sense of peace.

His father thinks, *Perhaps this is the child we have been waiting for.* "You may be right about her. She was raised to obey her husband, no matter what he asks of her. She doesn't know any better. However, you need to stop her from working soon." He picks up the empty cup, and hot coffee appears. He sips it slowly. "Are you certain she is the one?"

"Why does she need to stop working? And yes, Father, she is the one." James drinks a gulp of his coffee and stares at his father across the counter.

James's father rises from the counter, walks around to his son, and places both of his hands on either arm, peering into his son's eyes. He smiles. "You'll know soon enough, my boy! You will know soon enough. Until then, I want to meet her, so bring her by to meet your parents." He laughs in spite of it all. "How about tonight?"

James shakes his head. "I don't know, Dad. She has had a pretty full weekend already." Now he smiles as he flashes briefly back to them making love in the shower.

"Ah ha!" His father laughs and shakes his son's hand. "You have to know, I know everything, even know what you're thinking. Yes, I want to meet her tonight. I brought her a beautiful red dress and shoes; I think she is going to love them. I will look for you about five tonight." His father then vanishes into thin air.

"Dammit! I Hate it when he does that!" James worries about what tonight is going to yield as puts a cup of coffee together for Charity and takes it up the stairs to his sleeping beauty.

"Wakey, wakey, my beautiful baby! I brought you coffee," James says as he sits down next to me on the bed, gently moving my hair from my face. He places the coffee on the nightstand next to me and climbs back into bed, moving my hair back to see where he bit me yesterday. It looks like it has healed significantly overnight. Amazed, he rolls me toward him gently, kissing my shoulder. He pulls the front of my nightgown down to grasp my breasts, moving his head in to suck on one.

I smile with my eyes closed. "Oh Baby, what are you doing to me?" I say groggily.

"Loving my beautiful, soon-to-be wife." He smiles at me as he stops sucking and rests his head on the pillow next to me. "My father was here earlier. He wants to meet you tonight, so tonight will be 'meet the parents' night." He smiles again.

"Oh my God, I have nothing to wear! Oh honey. there's nothing open today!" I immediately go to roll out of bed, but he pulls me by my waist back in to bed, putting me back under the covers.

"My father took it upon himself to buy you something beautiful to wear, and shoes to match," he says while holding me to his chest.

"Huh? Um, okay. What color is it? Is it pretty?" I lean against him. "Do you like it? Do you think I will look good in it?" I am interrupted by his lips over mine.

"Baby, you could wear a paper bag and make that look sexy!" he says, kissing my lips and then all over my face, making me laugh.

"Honey, I'm scared. How are they? Are they mean? Should I act differently?" I bury my face in his chest again, worried.

"No worries. There is nothing that you can do or say that will surprise him. In my father's line of work, he is used to dealing with assholes." He looks up to the window and to the clouds. "So, what do you say we take our time in getting up?" He kisses my head full of blonde locks. "We will go about this day like normal."

"Okay. I am still nervous, though!" I say as I roll over and sip at my coffee. "Mmm, perfect!" I sit there for a minute and then turn toward him. "Thank you, baby!" He rolls over behind me, places his legs on either side of mine, hugs me from behind, and kisses my neck gently, slowly. "We are never going to leave this bedroom, are we?" I giggle a little while he kisses my neck.

"I just want you to know I love you, that's all."

"Oh, honey, I have been staring at my beautiful ring, thinking you couldn't have just bought this. Did you?"

"No. You see, I bought it two weeks before you ... well, I have had it a long time and knew I was only meant for you, only you." After grabbing my neck and pulling my face toward him, he kisses me, slowly running his tongue on my lower lip. "But you're mine now. You aren't going anywhere ever again."

Chapter 4

I have my dress on and am getting on my garter belt with the stockings. James comes upstairs to watch me. "Don't wear any panties. I want to be able to get at you whenever I want."

I look at him, worried. "But we are going to be at your parents' house! Won't they think bad of me if we do anything there?"

After walking up to me and backing me up against the bedroom wall, he kisses me and lifts me up against the wall. He wraps my legs around his waist. "Why do you think my father bought you the gown with the slit up the side? Easy access for me, whenever and wherever I want you."

I love his desire for me as I look him in his eyes, wanting him to take me right now. But he kisses me and slides me back to my feet.

"Damn, you are sexy! I love you in that!" He grins at me as he steps back, adjusting his now hard cock so that he can be more comfortable. "We have plenty of time for making love, but I told my father that we wouldn't be late."

"Okay, no panties," I say, sitting on the bed. I put on the beautiful red shoes.

"Now *that* is a gorgeous picture!" He grabs me and pulls me into him. "Okay, let's go meet my parents, Mrs. Angel!"

James makes sure that I wear the gorgeous coat he bought me—not that I wouldn't have worn it anyway. We get into his car and begin driving. I have no idea where we are going, and I am almost afraid to ask. I know it's pretty far away because we left at 3:30 p.m. for dinner to be served at five.

We seem to be driving forever when James reaches for my hand and says, "We're here."

We pull up to a huge gate. There is a man there who walks over to the car. "Oh nice to see you, Mr. Angel. I will open the gate immediately, sir!"

The gate opens, and the landscape is beautiful with the snow dusting the pine trees on our way up the lane. I squeeze James hand, and he smiles back at me.

We pull up to the most gorgeous mansion. It looks like a castle, and it's warm and very welcoming. My heart is pounding, and my chest begins to flush. Now I am really nervous.

James pulls up, and a valet comes to his door, "Mr. Angel, sir, I will take this for you!" James gets out of the car and runs around to my door. As he opens it, the snow is still falling. He helps me out, and I look around for a brief moment, admiring the snow falling lightly and the shimmer it has on the ground. It's so beautiful!

James smiles as he gently wraps my arm in his, helping me up the stairs. We just get to the door, and a woman opens the door. "Mr. Angel, how nice to see you and your beautiful fiancée! Your parents are in the great room. Please allow me to take your coats."

James helps me take off my beautiful coat, and he hands it to his father's servant. "Okay baby, let's go meet my parents!" he says with so much excitement in his voice that it shows all over his face. We begin to walk down the hall and past his father's den and into the great room. "Well, there they are! The happy couple!" James's father says as he walks over to me, reaching for my hand. I hand it to him, and he kisses it. "Well now, that gown is beautiful on you, my dear!"

"Oh my goodness, I am so sorry. Thank you so much for the gown, it is beautiful, and the shoes are just gorgeous! I wish I would have known you were downstairs when I was sleeping. I would have liked to have thanked you earlier!"

"Oh sweetheart, I just popped in on James unannounced. This is James's mother, Clarissa." Mr. Angel's wife is a red-haired beauty who is very stunning."

Looking at her, I am in awe of her beauty. "Oh my gosh. you're so pretty!" I snap out of my infatuation. "Um, thank you for such a wonderful son!"

She shakes my hand gently, saying, "Oh my, already?" Mr. Angel gives her a quick, piercing look. Clarissa then says, "Oh, I'm sorry, my dear. I am just caught off guard with your engagement, that's all."

Just as things are beginning to get uncomfortable, James comes up behind me and puts his arms around my waist. He gently caresses my belly. "Oh honey," I whisper to him. "That feels so good. Thank you."

The lady servant comes back into the room. Mr. Angel looks over at her. "Yes, Madrid?"

"Dinner is served, sirs and madams." Madrid then nods at him and exits the room.

"Shall we?" Mr. Angel his wife's arm and leads her into the dining room. James offers his arm to me, and I take it. We walk slowly toward the dining room, leaving some distance between his parents and us.

"Honey, what did she mean by that? Am I in trouble?" I ask.

"No, baby. I should tell you that my mother is psychic. I will ask her at dinner what she meant. Okay?"

"Really? Your mother is psychic? Oh wow, that is really great! I bet you probably didn't get a bump or bruise as a baby!" I joked to him.

We walk into a beautiful room, and I gaze around. The woodwork around me is absolutely stunning. The cherubs in the corner of the room are weeping. The mantle is gorgeous, and I can't stop looking around. I am a bit distracted while walking into the dining room with James. He walks me in very proudly, obviously happy that I have such an appreciation for things with history.

James pulls out my chair, and I sit down. The wait staff come around this beautiful table with dinner plates. It's steak done exactly the way I love it: Pittsburgh rare! It comes with Brussels sprouts and a baked sweet potato. What a beautiful presentation in a beautiful room, with wonderful company.

I am quiet but reach for James's hand. He grasps my hand, leans in, and kisses my cheek. I smile warmly back at him, so excited, Happy, and satisfied.

"So, Charity, I can see that you are in awe of my home. You know, James grew up here." Mr. Angel breaks the silence. He cuts his steak and puts a piece in his mouth.

"Oh, yes, sir! I love homes and buildings with history, especially woodwork. It shows a time when people took pride in the work they did."

Mr. Angel smiles at Clarissa, reaches for her hand, and squeezes it to let her know of his affection for her. "Clarissa picked the house, the furniture, and the woodwork. Whatever she wants, she gets. She's a good girl, my Clarissa." He winks at her. "As I am sure you are a good girl for our James."

"Yes, Father, she is my good girl. She knows what makes me happy and does whatever pleases me." James reaches for my hand again, and he now winks at me.

Dinner is finished, and we move into the den. James tells his parents that he wants to show me around the house. He takes my hand and walks me around this beautiful mansion. We walk to the stairs, which seem to wrap around to the upstairs … it's so hard to explain it. The banister is wood and gorgeous. The smell of this home is unique, perhaps even antique. James takes my hand, and we slowly walk up the stairs. There are many pictures and painted portraits on the walls. We are now on the second floor, and he takes me into a gorgeous room.

"This is the room that I grew up in—my bedroom," he says to me with a sly smile. "Come here, now." He uses a demanding voice. I quickly come to him, and he kisses me hard, picking me up and wrapping my legs around his hips. "This is why I said no panties. I want you when I want you, and how I want you." He unbuttons his slacks and forces his cock into my waiting pussy, pounding me hard and fast. I love it when he takes me, and I feel him inside of me. I love feeling desired and wanted as he does what he wants with me. He scratches my back, and this time I reach for his back and feel something strange as he is pounding me midair—some sort of humps in the middle of his back. I lean in and kiss him Deeply. His teeth tear my bottom lip a little, but I keep kissing him, bleeding and tasting my own blood. He kisses me harder, sucking my lip and my tongue. He pounds harder and harder, moving us toward his large four-poster bed. He lays me down gently on the bed, pulling my breasts out of the gown and holding on to them as reins.

"Oh, baby! Fuck me harder! I'm cumming!" I look up at him now, in his dominant glory—pounding me, wanting me, claiming me. I feel dirty and like a bad girl. I love being his bad girl!

He leans down to kiss me, and his eyes are all black! I think that this is my imagination as I kiss him. I'm turned on by the mere thought that he is magical, mysterious. "I love you!" he screams to me over our muffled kisses. He cums into my hot pussy with such force that I feel it deep within me. It makes me cum all over his thick girth!

Downstairs. James parents are sitting in the den. "I hear my boy up there breaking her in nicely! Very good girl, she is!" Mr. Angel says to Clarissa.

"You do realize she is pregnant, my lord," Clarissa says to her husband.

"Yes, my dear, I do. He has waited for her for the last 125 years. Don't you dare fuck this up again. Do you understand me?"

She bows to him. "Yes, my Lord." Then she walks toward the window, peering out. "They will have to stay the night. There is too much snow for them to travel."

"Ah, yes, ever faithful Mother Nature. Good, good!" He sits down in his reclining leather chair and puts up his feet. "Ah, that is comfortable. I can almost hear every breath they take together." He tilts his head back. "It's almost like music to my ears!" He smiles as fangs protrude from his lips, and his eyes are now blackened to their true form.

The wait staff enters into the great room, "Your cognac, my lord," Edgar says as he hands Mr. Angel a glass.

"Before you leave me, Edgar, ready a room for the children. They will be spending quite a few more days with us," Mr. Angel says in half of his true form.

"Yes, my lord," Edgar says, bowing as he leaves the room.

Upstairs, James and I lay next to each other on the bed. "I love you, baby," he says as he holds me tight to him with my head on his chest.

"I love you," I say. Every part of my body is pleased.

"Good. I want you to get on your knees and gag yourself on my cock."

"What? Aren't you tired, baby?" I lift my head to look into his eyes.

He quickly grabs my throat. "Did I not tell you to do something?" I nod to him as fear and excitement fill my body. My clit begins to throb.

I quickly rise to my knees on the bed and kneel with my ass toward his face. I begin to suck his long, hard rod. I love the way it feels in my mouth: full, soft, Long, and hard. I am sucking as he begins to finger my pussy and my ass. I suck harder, gagging myself on him, doing as he wishes and pleasing him.

He fingers me harder and deeper. "Mmm." He grabs the back of my head, forcing his cock down the back of my throat. "Yes! Suck my cock! Gag on me!"

Excitement and pain fill my body. I have no idea how many fingers he has buried in me. I don't care. I am feeling good and wonderful that I am pleasing him. He is making some guttural growling noise. I go to lift my head to look at him, but he shoves my head back on his cock.

"Did I tell you to stop! No! Now, suck my cock and gag until I cum down your throat!" He continues to force my head down on his cock, fucking my throat. He holds my head on his cock as he explodes his hot load down the back of my throat. I swallow it, but he keeps pumping his load down my throat. I take his full load. He lets up on my head so that I can lick his shaft and his head again. I then suck the head of his cock.

"I love how you do that! I love it when you serve me!" He is still fingering me, faster now. He grabs my hair and pulls me on top of his chest. "I want to watch you cum for me now!"

I don't know how he is doing it, but he is pulling my hair, fingering me, and pinching my nipples. I don't care. He is fingering me, pleasing me and himself. I can't help it. "I'm cumming! I'm cumming!"

His face changes, and his eyes are now black. His fangs protrude from his lips. "Keep cumming, baby! Don't stop!" He says as I stare into his face, cumming all over him. I can't stop and keep squirting! He pulls me into his face, kissing me. I am screaming in pleasure into his mouth, and he smiles at me with those eyes and fangs. But I don't care—I am so pleased and satisfied. I've never felt this way before.

He slides me off of his chest and onto the bed. "I know why my mother said what she said to you."

While lying there in awe of his form, I keep touching him, exhausted and very happy. My heart is still pounding, and I barely breathe the words. "Uh huh."

"Do you want to see me as I really am?" he says, looking at me staring and touching his body.

I stop for a moment. "You mean … it gets better?" He smiles at me with those beautiful teeth and fangs. He is still gorgeous, and I am his. "Yes. Yes, please," I say, looking into those black eyes.

"Stand up and get to the end of the bed," he says forcefully. I comply willingly with his request. He begins to tie my ankles to opposite sides of the bed, spreading apart both of my legs. He then ties my wrists to bedposts. I stand there next to him, naked and a little afraid.

"I told you I would show you what I truly look like." There is a huge sound almost like wings flapping, and then there's a loud thump. My heart begins to pound. There is heavy guttural breathing coming from behind me. His hands are no longer hands—they are clawed, almost talons. I try to keep from screaming in fear, knowing that he won't hurt me, but I can't stop the tears streaming down my face. I look back and see his eyes black of night staring back at me. He looks like a mutated gargoyle with large wings. His shoulders, neck, and chest are covered in muscles that flow down toward his buttocks and strong thighs.

He takes a few more steps toward me, wrapping his arms around me. I close my eyes and sigh in relief, knowing that it is truly him whom I love.

Still in his gargoyle-like form, he begins to touch me, first rubbing my breasts, caressing me slowly, and gently squeezing them. He makes me want him again. He then licks my neck, rubbing his head against mine. While feeling his breath against my neck, I can feel my own breath become shallow, and my heart pounds within my chest. I can feel my body want him. I want him! "Take me, take me now!"

"I love you," he says in a guttural voice. He comes up behind me, licking me from behind my neck all the way down to the crack of my ass. I'm so turned on by all of this, so wet. He slides his cock into my pussy—and another into my ass! I scream in pain and pleasure. He has each of his talon like hands on either side of my hips as he thrusts into me. I'm breaking into a sweat as he is pounding, thrusting, grinding, and growling, making love to me. I have never felt such a thing before. My body begins to tremble with excitement, and I am cumming at the same time. He can feel my insides getting tighter as I cum all over his cock. I can feel he is about to come as his cock gets bigger inside of me.

"Fuck me! Fuck me hard, baby!" I say. Hearing me scream this makes him pound me harder and faster until he lets out this shriek as I feel him fill me with his cum up both my ass and my pussy. Just as he's coming, his wings stretch out a full twelve feet in length and then fall to the floor, piercing the floorboard with some kind claw on either end. He wraps his arms around me, hugging me gently. He slides his long, taloned hands down my thighs, scratching me gently and turning me on all the more. My body is sore but satisfied. He unties me, ankles first and then my wrists. I fall into his arms, and he picks me up and carries me around the bed, laying me gently into the middle. He walks around the room and begins to stretch.

Slowly James begins to change back into his human form. His wings shrink into his back very naturally. His feet and legs turn human as he walks around the room, still stretching. After walking toward the window to peer out at the snow, he places both of his taloned hands on either side of the window, almost doing a push-up within the opening of the window. His back, buttocks, chest, arms, hands, neck, and head are human now.

He turns his head and sees his sleeping beauty on the bed. He smiles to himself, absolutely happy with his life. He is willing to die for her and will give her the world. She sighs deeply with a deep weight in his chest. He has the sudden urge to go to her, to hold her, to feel her within his grasp.

James slides into the bed and gets under the sheets, pulling me close. I feel the warmth of his body. Oh, how much I love him.

He then looks at me worriedly and says, "Are you okay?"

Exhausted, I open my eyes a little wider, looking over at him. "Oh honey, I'm fine—I'm more than fine. I love you. I have to admit, though I am a bit shocked that you have more than one … umm…" I smile at him. "In your demon form, but I still knew that it was still you making love to me."

James pulls me closer to him, still very sweaty from making love." Honey, I will never hurt you no matter what form I am in. And it's my Guardian form, similar to a gargoyle. Having two penises is called Diphallia. If I can't be satisfied more than a couple times a day or six times a week, it backs up in my prostrate—at least, that is what the doc says."

I try to open my eyes upon learning the most wonderful news any woman would love to hear. I act like my normal, smart-ass self. "'Hi, I want to be your husband. And oh, by the way, I have two fully functioning penises. Oh, by the way, I'm built like a Greek god. I have awesome wings and get free air fare. I have a slight discoloration problem, but no biggie.' That's great news, baby. So why did it take you so long to share all this with me, especially when you know I work with people who are really sick?" I can barely keep my eyes open, and I soon pass out from extreme exhaustion.

James smiles in spite of himself, thinking, I wanted and needed you to love me for me, not for my body. He laughs to himself as he pulls me to him. "Yup, she's my girl!" He holds me close to him, keeping me warm, happily knowing that I am all his from the day I took my first breath."

Our eyes close for the night, but little did I know that there was a child growing within my womb. Downstairs, James's father and mother sit at the fireside. Lou finishes his cognac, smiles, and says to his wife sitting across the room, "Yes, my dear wife, our little girl upstairs is going to work out just fine! She just saw our son in his truest form and didn't scream her head off. Rather, she had him fuck her eyes out!" He laughs to himself. "Our son is finally happy. He is finally home for good."

His wife sits there quietly, watching the fire dance on the logs and saying nothing. She keeps her thoughts to herself. What she is thinking is horrific at best.

Chapter 5

Waking up in James's warm arms has been wonderful. I wake up to the smell of coffee. He is still wrapped around me. I love this feeling, and I love his smell. *Oh my God, thank you!* I think to myself. *He is so good to me. he loves me. He doesn't hurt me. He holds me all night long.*

Just then, an overwhelming feeling of nausea overtake me. "Honey, I think I am going to be sick."

Groggily James wakes up. "Wha? Okay baby, let me get up and take you to the bathroom."

I sit there with one hand on my stomach and the other over my mouth, breathing deeply and slowly, and trying not to puke. "Honey, I'm sorry. I honestly—" I stop talking because it makes it worse.

James puts on his jeans and runs around the bed. He picks me up and wraps my in the sheet. He carries me into the bathroom, twenty feet from the bed. We get into the bathroom, and he sits me on the side of this beautiful bathtub that is sunken into the floor. He props me up against the cool wall. It feels good.

"Are you okay there, baby-doll?" he asks.

I nod, still holding my stomach and my mouth. I lean up against the wall; the cold wall makes me feel better and almost takes away the puking feeling. I look up at him. He is worriedly searching through drawers until he finds a washcloth. He turns on the water faucet, and I look at his gorgeous reflection in the mirror. He is strong and intent on assisting me. He now has the washcloth wet, and he wrings it out and comes back to me, opening it up long ways to put it on the back of my neck. He gently kisses my forehead. I smile at him as he takes the washcloth and gently wipes my face, dabbing it slowly. I put my hands over his and look at him. "I love you, James, so much. I love you."

"Honey, I have loved you for an eternity." He leans in to kiss me. He kisses my top lip and then stops himself. He smiles and leans back. "Um, not still, pukey, are we?" We both laugh.

"No. I think the coldness of the wall and this really pretty tub made me feel better."

James gets up and pushes a button on the wall.

The intercom squawks. "Yes, sir?"

"My wife isn't feeling well. Can you bring her some toast and ginger ale, please?"

"Right away, sir."

"Wow," I say, smiling up at him and readjusting my sheet across my breasts.

"Do you know how beautiful you are right now?"

"No." I feel very shy all of the sudden. My cheeks are warm and pink.

He walks back over to me, his naked chest muscular and gorgeous. His brown hair and his golden eyes complete his beautiful self. He smiles at me in those worn jeans with his bare feet. He is breathless to behold. He leans down and kisses me gently, sweeping me up into his arms once again as I bring my arm over his shoulder, revealing my breast to him. He smiles and kisses me gently, Beautifully, romantically.

"Let's get my baby dressed, before breakfast comes up."

He carries me back into the bedroom and sets me on the bed. After opening the drawers, he gets out some bootie socks, and a cute pair of sweatpants and a warm shirt. He sets the clothes next to me but then kneels and goes to open a pair of my bootie socks.

"Honey, what are you doing?" I ask, smiling awkwardly.

"You don't feel good. I just want to help you, baby. Let me help you." He looks up at me so sincerely that I can't say no. I willingly slide my foot toward his waiting, sock-filled hands. He gently slides the bootie sock onto my foot and gently massages my foot. It tickles a little, and I giggle. I lift up my other bare foot. He slides the other bootie sock on that foot, again massaging my foot and making me giggle.

"I love your laugh," he says as he stands and kisses me, pushing me back onto the bed as I wrap my naked legs around his hips. "Mmm, I love your lips, and looking into your eyes." He licks up my neck slowly. "And the way you taste. I love everything about you."

There is a knock at the door. "Just a minute," James says as he picks me up and places me in an upright position up against the headboard, covering me up. He quickly races for the door and opens it up.

A small cart wheels in. "I'll take it from here. Thanks," James says, smiling as he closes the door. I can't even see who was at the door. He lifts the lid and peers down at the steaming food. "Looks like they want to make sure you are going to eat." He moves the cart closer to the bedside as I readjust in bed. He sits close to me and lifts the lid, revealing breakfast for two: eggs over easy, toast with extra butter, sausage, ginger ale, and coffee—exactly the way we both like it.

"Here, honey, let's start slowly. Have a piece of toast." He hands me a piece of toast. I take it and begin to eat it slowly.

As I eat, I say, "I don't know what came over me this morning. Maybe all the excitement from all our extracurricular activities we have been having lately." I snicker, taking small pieces of bread and placing it in my mouth.

James folds his toast, dips it into his egg, and then pops it into his mouth. He chews and then swallows it before he speaks. "Honey, how would you feel if I asked you when you had your last menstrual cycle?" He observes me for a reaction.

I pause at first, not reacting so much as I am thinking. "I don't know. I haven't exactly paid attention. I'm sorry, baby."

James takes a sip of his coffee now, washing his food down as he swallows. He wipes his mouth with his napkin, slides closer, and puts his hand on my belly. I put my hand on his hand, looking at him and oblivious to what he is trying to insinuate. He is patient as he waits for this to sink in. He sits there, his hand on my belly, and now he smiles at me. I smile back at him reaching for the ginger ale. I sip it slowly.

"What, baby?" I finally say as I swallow my ginger ale, looking at him smiling at me with his hand still on my belly. "You think I can be …?"

He smiles very big now, moving so close that he is almost on top of me. He nods and holds my face with both of his hands. "Yes, baby, I do! I love you. I love you!" He kisses me all over my face.

"Honey, wait. I'm afraid. What if I'm not pregnant, and I disappoint you?"

He places his finger over my lips to quiet me. Tears begin to fill my eyes. "Do you remember the little comments my mother was making last night? My mother can feel some things. But I will ask my father to get our family doctor here and see how you are feeling. We won't say anything about pregnancy or babies, and we'll just see what he says. Okay?"

I'm willing to please the man I love with my entire being, my soul. I merely nod, tears now quietly streaming down my face. He wipes them away, kissing me softly and holding me close to him. "Baby, even if we aren't pregnant now, we will be. Or we will have a lot of fun trying!" He laughs, and I let out a little laugh as well. "Ah, that's my girl!"

I would do anything for him. I feel his heart beating as he holds me tightly against him. I have to stop crying now; I don't know what is coming over me. Why in the world am I so emotional?

James says, "Come on, let's finish getting ready." He kisses my forehead, and I watch him stand and walk over as he begins getting dressed again. James reaches into our overnight bag, handing me my sweatpants. I slide to the side of the bed, pulling them up my legs. I then put on my bra and adjust my breasts into each cup until I feel right. I can see him staring at me while I am adjusting my breasts. I smile back at him, almost embarrassed. I pull my shirt up over my head, and just as I pull it down over my face, James is standing in front of me, helping me pull it down the rest of the way. He kisses my lips, and I put my arms up around his neck and look ok into his eyes. "How did I get so lucky?" I say.

He wraps his arms around me. "I have been searching for you my whole life. Just you. You complete me." He pauses and says, "We have been upstairs most of the morning. Let's go find my father and get hold of that doctor to see if he will come out today."

We depart from the bedroom hand in hand, walking down the stairs to the great room. Lou is sitting in his chair reading the morning paper, drinking his coffee, and wearing his reading glasses. He hears us enter the room, and he immediately puts his paper down and folds up his glasses before walking toward us.

He reaches out toward me, taking my hands in his. "Good morning, my dear! I understand you woke up a bit under the weather, so I put in a call to our family doctor. He should be here within the hour." He looks at James. "I hope you don't mind ..."

James puts his arm around my waist, smiling at his father and then at me. "Thank you, Father. We were coming down to ask you that very thing."

"Oh, not a problem. After all, this lovely little beauty is family now, isn't she?" He gently squeezes my hands and then releases them, patting James on his shoulder as he returns to his chair.

"Have a seat, kids. Get comfortable. I have asked that they bring your lovely bride some ginger ale for her sickness, and some coffee for you."

James leads me to the couch. He sits, and then I sit and I put my feet up on the couch. He wraps his arms around me. A moment later, Madrid walks in with a warm blanket and wraps me up in it, carefully mothering me and smiling. She is so very kind to me. James kisses my head. "Thank you, Madrid. Thank you, Father, for everything."

I smile up at Madrid, peeking up over the blanket at her. She winks at me and smiles. "Coffee and Miss Charity's ginger ale is on its way, sir."

"Thank you, Madrid. Let us know when Dr. Seoul arrives," Lou says as he picks up his glasses and puts them back on.

Madrid nods and bows slightly, backs out a few steps, and turns and leaves the room.

James is complete, whole, sitting here with his father and the woman he loves. I can hear and feel the strength of his heart beating. He strengthens his grasp on me as I snuggle under the blanket a little closer to him. I peer over to his father, who looks up over his newspaper at the two of us, smiling. I wonder if he knows what his son is—or is Lou just like James?

Lou eventually breaks the silence. "Ah, James, I am so … pleased you found your baby, your girl!"

I can feel James's heart pounding as he clears his throat. "Thank you, Father. Thank you for helping me find her." He moves my hair from my face. "She's perfect," he says as he looks down at me, pausing one second and then looking up at his father with tears filling his eyes. "I think she's pregnant with my baby. She's all mine. They're all mine!"

Sensing he needs a big hug, I begin to shift myself to kiss him. His father walks up to him and hugs him as well. "Son, this is going to happen. Everything is going to be perfect—no more nightmares." He pulls James tear-filled face to look him in the eyes. Lou's eyes turn black, and he grows long fangs while looking down at his son. "What happened before will *not* happen again, trust me. I love you, my boy!"

James nods his head. pulling me into him so that I won't see the evil his father has just become. James trusts his father and loves him. He knows what happened over 131 years ago to his beautiful Celeste and his unborn child. Lou vowed that it would never happen again.

Madrid comes into the room. "I apologize, Master, but Doctor Seoul is here to see Miss Charity."

Lou looks at Madrid in his evil form briefly, and then he shakes his head and returns to his human form. "Please escort him in, Madrid. And please bring everyone's coffee and Charity's ginger ale."

"Immediately, sir." She bows slightly and leaves the room.

I adjust myself on the couch to sit myself on James's lap. "Baby, I'm okay. I just got a little sick, that's all. Maybe a little flu bug." I begin kissing his cheeks, Eyes, Forehead, and lips.

Madrid arrives moments later with Dr. Seoul. "So, this must be our little patient!" the doctor says as he enters the room, his arm reaching out to shake Lou's hand.

"How are you, Jack? How is the wife and kids?" Lou says heartily as he shakes Dr. Seoul's hand.

"Oh, the usual. The children are growing so fast, and so is the wife!" They both begin to laugh.

James shifts to stand up, and I move to make that possible. James stands up and reaches his hand out to the doctor.

"Jack, this is my boy, my son, my ... well, what can I say? He's my boy!" Lou pats James on his shoulder, grasping his shoulder and letting it go. James shakes the doctor's hand.

"Lou, your boy has your excellent grip! I'm wondering if he has your other qualities as well." He winks slightly at Lou.

I shift my position on the couch to get a little more comfortable; the nausea is coming back. I feel like I am about to puke, and just at that moment the doctor walks up to me and holds my head and neck. His hands are cold like ice, but it feels good; the nauseous feeling dissipates. I look up at him. I say, "Oh thank you. Thank you so much, Doc. can you figure out what kind of bug I've got in me and let me know how long I'm going to have it, so I know how long it's going to be before I start feeling better?"

James looks worried. Lou puts his hand on James shoulder, reassuring him. "Are you feeling better, baby?" James asks me.

I look over at him while the doctor starts to listen to my heartbeat, and I nod at him wearily and smile. The doctor listens to my belly. He opens up his bag and pulls out a sonar device, putting it to my belly. He turns it on, and it sounds like the ocean. I look up at James as the doctor moves it to another part of my belly. It sounds like a heartbeat; it's very fast. I put my hand up to my neck and feel my own heartbeat: mine is slow and steady. He moves it to another part of my belly, and there is another heartbeat. I put both of my hands up over my mouth and gasp, my eyes fill with tears. James jumps and runs over to me, smiling as tears run down his face. He kisses me all over.

"How? How can there be a heartbeat now? Are there *two* heartbeats?" I am confused but excited.

James is hugging me and kissing me as I look at him. He says, "I love you. So much!"

"That is impossible! I can't be ... I haven't been with *anyone*, not since the last time we... and that was almost a year ago! We only made love within the last couple of days." Panic takes over. as I look over at James. Not he nor anyone else in the room appears worried nor is questioning me in the least.

I look up at Lou. "How can this be? Is the baby growing fast because James is a ...?"

"A Guardian, my child," the doctor says very candidly while collecting his equipment.

Lou calls for Madrid. "Madrid, ready the downstairs bedroom for the children. I don't want Charity walking up and down the stairs."

James says, "Dad, that won't be necessary. I won't be leaving her alone, ever again." He mouths the words, *There are two babies now ... I can't lose them, any of them again,* He shakes his head, tears streaming down his face.

Lou watches his son's face and tearful plea, and then he turns to Madrid. "Madrid, run Charity a nice bath. and ready their room more permanently. They will be moving in, and Charity will be needing your midwifery services."

"Wonderful, sir. I knew the child was pregnant—the pheromones she was emitting were strong! She will be perfect for this baby!" Madrid says as she claps her hands together in excitement.

Quick to correct her, James says, "Babies. *Babies*, Madrid!" He happily pulls me into him.

Madrid pauses. "Two babies? My, my. Two angels!" She smiles and smacks her lips before pausing and pacing. "Yes, Yes," she says as she walks over to me lying on the couch with James. She touches my belly, looking at me and staring into my eyes. Then she stands upright and walks backward, tears streaming down her face. "She is reborn, my lord!"

Lou grabs Madrid. "Speak to me, Seer! What did you see?"

"I see ... an attempt is made to kill them again. Much despair, much pain—again!" she says as he has her in his grasp.

"Is it the same one?" Lou asks, shaking Madrid.

"Yes, Master, it is!" She is frightened.

James stands up, and I am getting scared. "Dad! I ripped him to shreds!" He stands there confused. "There was nothing left but scraps!" His fists are clenched, and his fangs protrude as he snarls.

Lou puts his hands on his son's shoulder, trying to calm the fury welling deep within him. "No, son, you didn't. But make no mistake, this is not a prophecy. This will not happen again!"

James says, "I told you, Father. She was the one. *Is* the one! I just knew it just had to be her!"

"Oh my God, James. I'm scared. Is someone going to hurt or kill me and our babies?" I say, frightened as tears stream down my face.

James looks at me and picks me up off of the couch, cradling me. "I'm going to protect my wife, my family, even if I have to go across the planet and not tell a living soul!" He sweeps me around and begins to take me up the stairs as a feeling of overwhelming fear takes over. He climbs the staircase, muttering to me. "No one is going to hurt you or my babies, honey. No one! I will keep you safe!"

We make it to our room. There are beautiful flowers everywhere. James sets me down on the bed. He pulls the shades, but not before he peers out the window, looking for a sign that someone or something may be coming uninvited.

I peer around the room. Madrid must have brought us something to eat because there is still food and drink in a warmer in the corner of the bedroom. It catches James's eye. He walks over and pours me a small glass of ginger ale, walking to my bedside as he sits and gently hands it to me.

I look at him, tears still filling my eyes and streaming down. I am trying to believe he can protect me, protect us … but what if? I take a sip as he sits there looking at me. determined to protect us from whatever may be out there.

He tries to smile at me. "How's my baby? Oh, sorry." He gently puts his hand on my belly. "Babies? How are my babies?"

I turn and put the glass down on the nightstand before I reach out for him to hug me. He quickly embraces me; neither of us says a word.

I can feel the warmth of his body and his breathing on my neck and slightly down my back. I know he wants to be strong for us, but I need to find out what happened before I was in the picture.

"Come on, baby. Madrid must have brought some food up for us to have lunch here together, since you weren't feeling well," he says while still embracing me. He slowly slides back to rise from the bed. He walks over to the corner of the room where the hot food is and begins to put the food on two plates. His steak is almost cooked, not exactly the way he likes it, but it's meat nonetheless. Madrid made fluffy scrambled eggs for me, probably because it will be light on my stomach. I love watching him. He is so careful, so sexy, in that form-fitting T-shirt from his shop, Angel's Automotive. It's black and squeezes his muscular arms in such a way that it makes me bite my lip.

James turns to me, almost in slow motion. he smiles, knowing that I am admiring him. He is watching me just as I am watching him, and he is looking for my grand finale: I lick my lower lip slowly when I am about to snap out of whatever self-induced love trance I put myself in. He is walking toward me Slowly, and now he is almost upon me. He puts my plate down at my left and sets his on the bed. "And there it is," he announces in a slow, gentle voice. He lifts my chin, kissing my bottom lip.

"Mmm, baby, I love that! You're so damn sexy!" I say as he slowly releases my chin and gets himself settled on the bed. We eat, and James almost inhales his food. I love watching him eat. I love the way he devours his food; it's almost the way he devours me when we make love.

"Do you feel any better, baby?" he asks, lifting the plate off of my lap and walking it back to the corner of the room.

"Yeah, but I could go for a nap. Wanna join me?" I playfully pat the side of the bed next to me.

"Oh hell yeah!" He quickly blows out the chafing lamps under the food and then takes a nose dive from the end of the large bed to the pillow. I let out a giggle as he rolls me onto his body. My hair falls down, shadowing my face. He gently slides my blonde locks behind my ear. "I love you so much. Nothing is going to happen to you. We'll stay here, at home with my parents. We'll be the safest."

I nod at him. I love the way he makes me feel. I close my eyes for a moment as he slides his fingers through my hair and onto my scalp. I open my eyes slowly. He pulls my mouth to meet with his, kissing me passionately and deeply, with even more fire. He slowly rolls on top of me, having more control over my body. I sigh, wanting him. He is kissing me and running his hands up my shirt, grasping my breast. "I can't seem to get enough of you."

I wrap my legs around his hips and slide one down the back of his leg, looking at this beautiful, sexy, strong man. "I don't want you to. I am yours, all yours. I belong to you."

Listening to my words leave my lips, he puts my arms up over my head with one hand, holding them there. "You are mine! You *do* belong to me! You always have! Since the day you were born, you belonged to me, baby!"

I look up into his eyes, intent with love, lust, and fury—all for me. I lift my head up and kiss him furiously. He begins to strip off my clothes as I reach and help him take off his.

I live every day to make him happy and to love him. Making love to him is a bonus.

Downstairs, Dr. Seoul sits down on the couch, peering across the room at Lou. "Lou, you know that jealous witch of yours has to be dealt with. James cannot continue to suffer like this! I am amazed she didn't try to kill your son, the minute he burst from her and took his first breath!"

Madrid stood over by the fireplace, staring into the fire. She now says, "I will have to bind her from entering their room, or any room that they are in." She turns away from the fire, joining the two men in the room.

"It's not going to work. She will enchant someone to do her bidding. I warned her. I *warned her*. not to hurt the child again, either of them! And yet she defies me again!"

"So what do you want to do, Lou?" the doctor asks.

"The only thing that must be done. She must die!" he says as he changes into his full demon form. He is much taller than James with dark black wings. His face is strong, and he has a profound jaw line. Remarkable, large horns protrude from his head. His teeth and fangs are large, and his eyes are blacker than midnight. His body is muscular and without a doubt unlike any other, for he is the king, the master of all.

He looks at his two servants now bowing before him. "Get me Clarissa, now!"

They both rise and depart.

"Jack, I want you to come back and take care of Charity and the babies. I want her comfortable." As he begins to calm down, he changes back into his human form. "Oh, before I forget, is there anything that can be done about her morning sickness?"

"Yes, my Lord. Keep giving her the ginger ale. Keep her fed and bathed. Your son will not be able to resist her pheromones," he says, smiling out of the corner of his mouth.

"Ah. My boy … I think she can handle him. She has already experienced him in his form, but I will make him aware to be a little careful." He smiles to himself. "Thank you, Jack, for everything." He shakes the doctor's hand. "I look forward to seeing more of you around here."

"I will be here first thing in the morning to set up all the equipment I will need to monitor her pregnancy from here, so that there will be no risk that Clarissa will reach her."

"Thank you. I look forward to it."

Jack leaves, and Lou turns to the fireplace, staring into the flames. He calls into the flames. "Daemonum autem opportuno accersam te. Protege filium meum, et uxor ejus a partui. Oratio Clarissa et uxor tua, me. You iubet."

A demonic face appears out of the flames. "Sic faciemus tibi, Magister."

Lou smiles and waves him away. Madrid enters the room with a cognac for her master.

"Impeccable timing, my dear!" he says as he takes the cognac from her tray. "How does their room look Madrid? Did you make it look beautiful and homey?" he asks while sipping at the glass and walking toward his chair.

"Yes, I did, but they are sleeping in James's childhood room tonight."

"The good doctor will be back tomorrow. He will be making one of the bedrooms a labor and delivery suite, and he will be bringing plenty of equipment tomorrow. See to it that everything runs smoothly."

"I will, my Lord." She bows and turns to leave.

"Madrid, there may be another way, a way that I can save my family, and not have to kill my wife."

"I think I remember, my lord. I will work on that." She leaves the room, closing the doors behind her.

Lou sits in his chair by the fireplace, where he can feel the exquisite warmth of the fire. He goes to sip his cognac but is interrupted by the sounds of light thumping upstairs, coming from James's bedroom. He smiles and lets out a small chuckle, "Yup, that girl is going to give that boy a run for his money!" He laughs again and sips his cognac slowly, watching the fire do a dance almost like a ballet of sorts. He listens to the rhythmic thumping combined with the dance of the flame, watching it dances its heart out, swaying and leaping from log to log, being caught by another flame and pirouetted until it appears as though the flamed dancers have lost their fiery energy till the very end of the performance. It almost makes him want to stand up and applaud.

Chapter 6

I lay in James arms. warm and safe. I close my eyes and begin to dream. At first I am in the woods, running with many leaves and broken branches beneath my feet. I am rushing to get there, to a little cottage buried in the woods. I make it! While breathing heavily, I close the door behind me, locking it securely. I peer out the small window. This cottage is a place I am unfamiliar with, but I feel as though I am.

I walk around the room, and it is homey and warm, not as damp as I first thought it to be upon entering. I feed the fire with logs. I am looking for James.

I begin to tidy up this place and make soup. I seem to know what I am doing because the vegetables are already in a bowl on the table with a hanging pot. I chop the vegetables and notice that there is no meat for the soup. That must be where he is right now.

I bump myself on the corner of a chair, and I notice that I am pregnant—very pregnant. My water breaks! Almost immediately I am in pain, buckled over and screaming for James. Everything is moving in slow motion. I make it to a bed, sweating, and I begin to peel off some of my clothing.

There's a knock at the door, but I can't get to it. I'm screaming for them to help me. This shadow knocks down the door, takes me out of the cottage, and holds me up by my throat. I hear a woman's voice coming from behind me. I can feel this baby wanting to leave my body—now. I am in such pain. Then the woman's voice behind me says, "Child of Christ, vessel of the devil! No more!" I feel this piercing pain in my back and through my chest. A long knife plunges through my heart and out my chest. The man throws me onto the ground like garbage.

A tear rolls out of my eye and down my face. I will never feel his embrace again, his beautiful kisses, or how much he loved us. Ever again. I lay there on the cold ground as they all saddle up and ride away leaving me to my death.

I am sitting there as a spirit, watching myself, lifeless. The child we were supposed to have pours from my body. I begin to sob. The child's spirit now stands with me; It is a little boy. Jacob. "Mommy, why did they do that?" he asks.

"I do not know, my love, but we will sit here until your father finds us. I feel he is near."

"Celeste! Celeste!" He is running through the woods almost in a panic, picking up her scent as well as the scents of horses and men.

He smells the scent of blood and fear, and of his Celeste. He runs quickly and comes upon his love's lifeless body, and that of their child.

"Oh my God! Celeste! Why?" He picks her up in his arms, and then his beautiful baby, placing him on her empty womb. He lifts them up, tearful.

I am still standing there with Jacob. I am not me. I am "Celeste," and this was their child. I am still holding onto this child's delicate hand. He looks at his father Sobbing and holding our lifeless bodies in his arms.

My love's form begins to change. He begins to scream, and it's guttural, primal. Wings flash out of his back quickly, black as night, as his whole form changes. He is still crying and enraged, and he takes flight with the lifeless bodies of his family, headed for his father.

I wake myself from this terrible dream, in tears. James is there with me. He wakes up, pulling me into him. "What's the matter, baby?"

"I just had a bad dream." I wipe the tears from my eyes and cheeks.

He kisses my head. "Tell me about your dream."

I tell him exactly what I saw in my dream. He wakes up almost immediately. "Baby, you said you saw this in a dream?" He Is holding me close to him and looking up at the ceiling.

"Yes. I felt like I was there. Then this little child and I went hand in hand into the light as you took flight."

Tears begin to fill James's eyes and quietly stroll down his strong features. He remembers that day. He will never forget that day. his heart was ripped out from his chest, and he was forced to walk the earth alone, saddened forever by the loss.

"It's all right baby. Get some sleep. I love you. Nothing is going to happen to you," he says as he squeezes me close to his chest.

James closes his eyes and begins to dream. Everyone within the walls of the mansion begins to dream. Everyone is brought back to that fateful day, the day where everyone's life changed. Strangely enough, everyone is reliving their own moments in time.

James is brought back to that moment, that time when his heart was destroyed and his life was changed. He can almost smell their blood in his dream. He knows this day. It was the day he flew his beloved Celeste's lifeless body and his sweet, innocent Jacob to his father.

James lands on the long hall of the keep of his father's castle in the mountains. He kicks in the doors and enters. Everyone who is in the hall at that time is alarmed and begins to run in a panic. His father's aides run immediately to take the lifeless bodies from James. Madrid runs quickly down the aisle to the lifeless Celeste and tiny Jacob.

As the aides lay the bodies on the carpet, Madrid knees down places her hands on their chests and then their heads. She looks up at the king, tears welling in her eyes. "They've been gone too long, my lord. Celeste suffered much!"

"I want to find and rip their murderer to pieces, Father!" James growls.

Lou steps down from his throne, approaching the two children lying lifeless, grey, cold. "Argh. Beautiful babies! Madrid, who has done this?" he says to her quietly."

She looks at him and shakes her head, her eyes, still streaming with tears. "My lord, we know who has done this terrible thing." She mouths these words to him silently.

Angered, he rises to his feet to approach his heartbroken, bloodthirsty son. "Son, seek out who it was, all of them, and rip them to shreds. Leave nothing for their families to bury."

Angry and anxious. James stomps over to his wife and child. kneeling at their side. He gently picks up Celeste's head, kissing her lips. Tears stream down his face and onto her cheek. He gently lays her head back down and picks up his tiny child in his large hands. He puts his forehead to his child's, kissing his tiny little nose and then his head. Then he lays the tiny baby on his wife's empty womb. He looks around the room silently, tearfully, seeing all the faces around him in tears, sharing in his grief. He turns slowly away from his family storming toward the doors, and then he abruptly takes flight, shrieking into the night sky.

Madrid sits with the lifeless bodies and begins to rise to her feet. "Come." She waves to many of her subjects. "Gather a blanket and take the princess and the young prince to be readied for burial."

Many rush quickly at her behest. They gently lift Celeste and Jacob and usher them off to be prepared for burial. Many are in tears while lifting their lifeless bodies. Madrid clears the large hall. She is now alone with the king, bowing in his presence, "My lord, we know who has done such a thing! What if James finds out it was his own mother?"

"He will only pick up the scent of her henchmen. She isn't that stupid," Lou says, utterly disgusted. "Oh what are we going to do with my dear, beloved wife!" He adds angrily as he begins to rise from his seat.

Madrid, weary with grief, looks up at the king, "The child won't be reborn again for another ninety-five years. James will be forced to walk alone for ninety-five years without his love. He has to live to fulfill his destiny."

Angry and infuriated, Lou storms past Madrid and toward the open doors his son has exited. He screams into the night, "Clarissa! Damn you!" He then looks back at Madrid and points at her, tears streaming down his face. "You must turn him to stone. He cannot be without her. he cannot suffer forever! We will have to turn him after he rips the bastards to shreds! Let him think he has gotten his justice but do not let him get too close to who it really is." Lou fearful of what the future holds, and he sighs deeply. "Please. Work on a spell and come to me when you have it perfected for both of these children."

Madrid rises to her feet, bows, and then exits. No words are spoken.

Chapter 7

James is flying through the woods in his gargoyle form. He lands in the exact spot he found his murdered family and picks up various scents of many men. He sees a pair of footprints still fresh in his wife's blood and amniotic fluid. He puts his face to the ground to mark this scent into his memory. This scent is familiar to him—he knows this scent. He sits down and begins to filter through every scent of everyone he has ever marked in his memory. Many faces filter through his mind like fragments, and then he sees a face. *Lucas!*

James immediately gets to his feet and growls, fists clenched. His wings spread out, and he takes flight to Lucas's cottage. He hears Lucas laughing inside. James decides to be smart about luring him out and goes behind his cottage. change back into his human form. He starts banging on the door of the cottage.

Lucas answers the door, drunk on wine. "James? What brings you here?" the man says, trying to sound concerned.

"I cannot find my Celeste! There is so much blood! I cannot find her! I am afraid for her and my baby. will you help me, brother? Please?"

James looks convincingly worried, summoning tears to the surface when thinking of his beautiful wife's lifeless body.

"Yes! Yes, Brother, I will help you find her!" Lucas looks back at his wife. "I am going to help find Celeste with James. I will return soon!" he leaves his home, closing the door behind him.

"Thank you, brother! It looks as though she was dragged, and then nothing! I can't even pick up a scent!" Tears still stream down his face.

"It looks as though you fear the worst, brother," Lucas says as he makes his way up the long hill and into the woods with James.

They are getting closer to where Celeste was murdered. The woods are deep and dark, but fortunately there is light from the full moon. They are finally upon James's cottage. James fantasizes for a moment, imagining Celeste running out the door and up to him, jumping up into him, her arms around him. She is kissing him, loving him, And smiling, her long blonde hair glistening in the morning sun. James stops walking for a minute, closing his eyes and trying to imagine her saying, "I love you," just one more time ... but he is interrupted by Lucas.

"Hey, are you picking something up?"

"Yes, you can say that," James says under his breath.

"What?"

"Nothing. I'm not picking anything up. Do you see anything, brother?"

Lucas turns and walks toward where he left Celeste's lifeless body. James walks slowly behind Lucas. With every step, he changes more into his gargoyle form.

Lucas is at the exact spot where he dropped Celeste after she was killed. He squats to look as though he is tracking some aspect of where she may have been killed, Dragged, or whatever it was that James said might have happened. He is trying to figure out what he is going to say when he stands and turns around.

James is standing upon him in his full gargoyle form.

Lucas yells, "Oh my God! James!"

James picks him up by his throat and throws him into the trunk of a tree. Lucas's body slams hard into it and falls to the ground. James storms over to Lucas and picks him up again.

"James! James, please!" Lucas pleads, coughing up blood.

James brings Lucas's face up to his, snarling as he speaks. "Is that what my beautiful angel did? Plead for her life—to you?" He throws his body back to the ground. "I am going to know who all was involved with this. You will tell me!"

"I can't. I can't! my whole family will be …"

James senses that Lucas is dying. Slowly James stomps toward Lucas. "If you do not tell me, I will rip them apart myself—as I will you!"

"I will tell you nothing," Lucas manages, coughing up more blood and smiling at James. "By the way, your bitch was giving birth to your bastard as I dragged her out of your bed to this spot. And yes, I enjoyed killing her! She should have been mine!"

James, consumed with rage, lifted Lucas up by his throat, his wings spread wide. Claws outside of his wings come out and stab Lucas in his shoulders, holding Lucas up in front of him. James punches his fist quickly into the man's chest, ripping out his still beating heart and showing it to Lucas. He sees the look of terror on Lucas's face. James rips Lucas's head off without blinking, screaming into the sky. He leaves his body but takes his head with him as blood trails away from his body.

James flies to his father's castle with Lucas's head in his grasp. He lands on the patio and walks into the long hall. His father is sitting on his throne, awaiting his son's arrival. James storms in, covered in Lucas's blood while carrying his head.

"Who is that? Lucas? Lucas murdered Celeste?" Lou says, looking perplexed at James.

"His footprints were covered in her blood and amniotic fluid, Father. He didn't deny it! He said he *enjoyed* killing my angel!" Snarling, James slams Lucas's head to the marble floor so hard that brain and bone shatter everywhere.

"James, okay. Please, son … Madrid has prepared your family. Go be with them. Heal your heart."

James falls to his knees, changing slowly back into his human form, Sobbing and looking up at his father. "They're gone forever! I will never hear my son breathe, or my beautiful angel say she loves me! Why am I being punished?" He is still sobbing.

The king, stricken with grief himself over his son's extreme loss, pains his heart, and he also falls to his knees, wrapping his arms around his son, holding him and allowing him to weep. James calms down after some time. The king is the father he always was to his son: a loving father, a good ruler, a fair man, always trying to strive to work his way back into the graces of his own father. "Son, let's get you to your family so that you can say your good-byes."

James has no words left in him, or strength. He needs his father to help him to his feet. His father walks with him to the chapel. After opening the doors, they both walk in. Celeste and tiny Jacob are lying there, dressed and perfect.

James looks at his father. "They look like they are sleeping." He examines their bodies, almost hopeful.

"They're gone, son. I'm sorry," Lou says softly, still holding James's shoulder. Sensing that James needs his time alone to grieve, he slowly leaves his son's side, backing out slowly and closing the doors behind him.

James, sensing he is alone, climbs up beside his beautiful angel, sobbing. He is careful not to disturb their perfection. He places his arm on her now flat belly. His fingertips touch his son's tiny, delicate foot carefully nestled in Celeste's left arm. He touches his foot, running his finger slowly up his fragile heel to his tiny, pink toes. "I'm so sorry, baby. I am so sorry I wasn't there to protect you both from them." He reaches for her soft blonde hair and brings it to his nose, burning her scent into his memory. He softly sobs to himself. "I feel like I am dying without you. I would give anything just to hear you tell me you love me, to feel the warmth of your body, to feel your belly grow and move once again." He sobs softly to himself. placing his arm over her again gently, trying to hold on to any moment he has left to touch her, and to touch the perfect child he will never hear cry or watch grow.

Sensing his son's extreme pain. and loss, Lou is so angry that he storms into his wife's room. "Where were you this morning?"

She sits at a mirror. brushing her long red hair. "What do you mean?"

He stares at her in the mirror, enraged by her avoidance. He grabs her by the hair, spinning her around, lifting her up, and holding her against the wall. "What did you do, witch!" He snarls as his fangs protrude from his lips.

She finally says, "I stabbed that whore. And killed them both!"

"*Why?*" He drops her back to her feet but still holds her up against the wall.

"We are supposed to have our time. Our *future*. Our destiny!"

"Bitch! You killed our son—his future, his destiny! You treacherous …" He stops short, letting go of her throat and pacing away from her. "I will fix this somehow, some way. And when I do, should you interfere in any way, I will kill you. Mark my words, witch. I have lost all love for you at this moment!"

"You never loved me!" she lashes out at him.

"Clarissa." He walks up to her, turning her toward him. "There was nothing I didn't love about you. Your beautiful smile, your voice, your giggle when I would tickle you. Especially everything you went through to give me a child—our son. The son you just killed with your meaningless jealousy!"

Seeing the anguish in his face delighted her. She turns away quickly; she doesn't want him to see her delight in his pain. "What can I do to help you fix this?" she says, attempting to sound concerned.

"Keep your distance from me and our son. That is what you will do. the sight of you disgusts me!" He storms out of her room, slamming the door behind him.

She sits back at her mirror, Smiling and combing her tussled hair. "I will have my destiny, and it doesn't include any of them." She laughs to herself.

The king seeks out Madrid and finds her in the kitchen. He says, "Can you feel his pain? His sorrow?" He stares into her eyes, searching for a response.

"Yes, my lord. I sense the boy's pain. I have researched my spell, but I can only place the boy in stone for ninety-five years, and he must be in his full Guardian form for him to survive."

"What will we tell him to instigate the full Guardian form?" he asks while sitting at the table with Madrid.

"He must protect the souls of his family so that they not be corrupted by evil. As the bodies of Celeste and Jacob are committed to the mausoleum, he shall take his place outside to protect them." While saying this, she writes more words on her scroll.

"Brilliant, and terrifyingly true!"

Silence fills the room. Lou then says, "The children will be committed to the mausoleum in the morning. as will my son. Then you and I will figure out what we will do with Clarissa. Get some rest, Madrid. We will need our strength tomorrow. Many an emotion we will endure in the morning." With a heavy heart he rises from his seat, patting Madrid on her shoulder as she touches his hand gently. Their eyes lock only for a moment, and then the king takes his leave.

Dawn

An hour before dawn, Madrid comes to wake the young James. She comes into the chapel and sees him lying next to his young bride and tiny baby. She stops dead in her steps, choking back tears and knowing what could have been, what was for him, what was for the entire kingdom. Now, she knows what must be done to protect him, to give him a second chance with the one he loves and deserves, and the destiny he … no. They were supposed to fulfill it together.

Her heart pounds out of her chest, and tears stream down her face. She sobs quietly to herself and gasps for air to breathe. The sight of this dreadful yet so very loving, sad, heartbreaking sight is enough to shake even an old seer to her foundations.

She takes another breath and wipes the tears from her face. She cannot hide her pain and anguish over this sight. She steps toward James lying there holding his family, quietly breathing, almost like he is curled into them. *Oh how painful this is to see, to feel. There is so much pain and loss in this room; it emanates from every crevice of every mortar and stone.*

She is finally upon James and sees his face stained in the tears that he has been crying all night long. She places a hand on his shoulder.

"I can't leave them, Madrid," he says softly.

"You don't have to. I have come up with a spell, but I need to speak to you about it first." She has a quiet, hopeful sound in her voice.

James opens his eyes and carefully moves his hand from his wife and son. He shifts his body to face her. "How? What is it that I need to do?"

"In order to meet again, you have to watch over their souls for ninety-five years. At the end of that time, you will both be reunited again, but she will not remember you. You will have to make her love you all over again. There are risks involved, James." There is caution in her voice.

He turns his head gently to look back at his sleeping bride. So gentle, so beautiful, so fragile. Her love was so great and deep for him. He looks back at Madrid and sighs deeply. "What must I do? I will do anything." Tears beginning to stream down his face again, for he knows what she is about to ask him to do. It is what most Guardians are asked to do, but this is the ultimate sacrifice. There may be no coming back from it.

"You must become your full Guardian form, your most fierce—full armor, sword, and all, ready for battle. In order for this to work, you must be committed shortly after your family is committed to the mausoleum."

His eyes peer into hers. "Madrid, there is something you're not telling me, isn't there?" He is questioning her, perhaps her motives.

"Yes, but I cannot tell you more. All I can do is protect you. All your father can do is protect you." She redirects his attentions immediately to the urgency. "James, if you wish to have another chance with her, you must hurry. Armor up and meet the processional outside as soon as possible. Tell no one ... I mean, tell No one."

The look of intent on her face is enough to let James know that something is going on. She can't say but needs him to be prepared to fight—and fight he will for the love of his life. He pauses a moment to kiss his beautiful Celeste on her head once more, and perhaps for the last time. He storms off to ready himself for what the battle he may have to fight: the battle for love, a true Guardian's battle.

Madrid stands alone with the bodies of the children, walking to touch the heads of the two at once. She sighs and takes a candle out of her apron. She lights it from one of the lanterns on the tables against the wall. Slowly she walks toward the two lifeless bodies, careful not to allow the flame to go out. She stands at the heads of the two and places the candle at Celeste's head. After rubbing her hands together, she closes her eyes, raises her hands, and in a commanding voice says the words.

Ariel begins it.
Baradiel guides it.
The Chalkydri sing it.
Devas manifest it.
Elohim wills it.
The Fravashi better it.
Gabriel brings it.

The Hafaza watch it.
The Ischim balance it.
Jael guards it.
Kadmiel births it.
Lahabiel aids it.
Michael raises it.
Nebo ministers it.
Ofaniel sees it.
Patron angels devote it.
The Queen of angels speaks it.
Raphael inspires it.
Sandalphon prays it.
Thrones sanctify it.
Uriel strengthens it.
Vrevoil reveals it.
Watchers protect it.
Xathanael patrons it.
Yahriel places the glory of the moon on it.
Zodiac angels seal it.
And Spirit brings it through time and space

She says this over and over again until the Angel Gabriel appears as the candle blows out. Gabriel looks at the children lying on the platform. "Why does the witch still live?" he asks.

"She will be dealt with. Your brother will deal with her appropriately."

"James is willing to sacrifice the next ninety-five years to usher in the new world?"

"Yes. He will do anything for his love. he loved them, Gabriel. He loved them with his entire soul."

"Then I will undo what was done, but she will not know him. He will have to work harder with the next one."

She smiles at his graciousness. "I understand, as he will. As does your brother. He is making the ultimate sacrifice too."

Gabriel touches the head of Celeste and of tiny Jacob, and he closes his eyes a moment. In a most powerful voice he states, "Then it will be done!" Just as quick and swiftly as Gabriel was summoned. he disappears.

Moments later there is a knock at the door. The ushers enter the room. "Madrid, my lady, we are ready."

"What of the king?"

"He is ready, as is James."

"Then let us proceed."

It is just starting to rain. The clouds are starting to gather around the castle. The two bodies are covered by a sheer sheath that is clear for all to see them in their final journey to eternity. This is the longest walk in the rain that James has ever endured. Though he has faced many a battle, fought many men and beasts, he has never felt so empty with an ache so deep in his heart. It is a bottomless pit of despair.

Finally they make it to the mausoleum and enter. James looks up and sees that his mother is missing. "Father," James whispers, "where is Mother? She should be here to send my family off to the promised land."

The king chokes back his discontent. "She is not well today, my son. Come now," he replies in a somber tone, ushering James along.

All sit, and Lou says a small sermon. "My father states that 'he who believes in him shall have everlasting life. This young, beautiful little girl most certainly believed in the Almighty God. She was her own little ray of beauty and sunshine. She blessed her and my son with little Jacob, soon to be born unto this Earthly plane. He would have grown to change the world. But now we commit their souls to the heavenly gates and hope that one day we shall all be reunited. So, Father, please take great care of them. We shall always love and miss them with great reverence." Lou steps down.

James steps up and places a calla lily under Celeste's hand, kissing her on her head one last time. Then he takes his place by his father's side.

They sit and watch the procession of grieving visitors pay their respects to the most beautiful and warm woman in the world. Then they leave to meet the king and James outside.

Finally, the last individual came and went. Father stood, as did he. Father turned to James midway down the aisle. "Are you prepared to spend eternity with them, to protect their souls?"

James stands tall and proud. "I have never been more sure about anything in my life, Father. I love them that much!"

"Then it will be done." Father puts both of his hands on either of James arms and pulls his body into his. Tears streaming down his face. "I love you, and I am proud of you."

They emerge from the mausoleum only to see that the castle, including this area, is surrounded by angels. James, feeling guarded, Nervous, and somewhat angered by this unprovoked turn of events. I looked to Madrid. "What is this? What is happening here?"

"Hurry, James. Remember what we spoke of earlier?" she says.

"Yes."

"It is now or never, James. The twenty-six angels are here to protect us from the evil that is trying to stop the spell from happening."

James looks around and sees all the angels he has come to know, including his father. His own father has now transformed into his true form. Feeling safe, he looks to Madrid and to the sky. He yells, "For you, my love!"

James changes into his full Guardian form. His wings spread out full and his sword is raised high. His teeth are full form, his eyes are black as night, and he has a full, muscular form rivaled only by the statues of the Greek god Adonis. He is truly a powerful, menacing presence. Madrid feels like there is no shred of humanity left within him at this moment, only the Guardian. She begins to read the spell.

> Time, stand still, till the ninety-fifth year.
> I cast this Guardian into stone, to be protected as he has protected,

Until the child's first cry is heard upon the earth.
Time, stand still until his destined love is reborn.
I command you. It is as it was supposed to be, and will be again!

Madrid blows sage and ash toward James as he roars in pain. He arches up into the striking position as his body begins to turn grey and then white in a wave across his body as he transforms to a hardened stone. Tears stream down Madrid's face and also the faces of many of the townspeople; they know why he has done this. The angels bow their heads in reverence. Gabriel and Michael come to the front of the mausoleum where James has just been turned to stone, and they stand with Lou. The three look upon the kingdom. Gabriel stands with a wooden clock in his hands, signaling to the other angels to sing the lullaby of time. Gabriel sings, his hand holding the second hand in place throughout the entire song.

Lou witnesses his son, his life, cast into a hard and lifeless stone. He roars in his gargoyle form, whipping his tail and slamming it on the ground. His fists are clenched. He hears his Clarissa in the distance, from her window. Now distracted from his grief, he begins to change to his human form for the sake of not just his townspeople but for Clarissa as well.

Inside the castle, Clarissa hears the lullaby of time being chanted. "What? No!" She leaves her couch to run out her bedroom, in an attempt to reach the king. she is blocked from moving beyond her room. She opens her bedroom door and goes to run out, but it was as though she hits an invisible wall. After hitting the wall, she falls to the ground, screaming in anger! "Damn you! No!"

The twenty-six angels continue to chant. Just then, the moon and the sun seem to share the sky. Gabriel looks at Lou and says, "This lullaby will age everyone one day for every ten. It will last for the next 120 years." He hands Lou the clock. "You must hang this in the highest steeple of the castle and keep it safe. Time will speed up slowly and naturally the closer that it gets to when the child will be reborn, and then James will be returned to you."

Michael interrupts Gabriel. "James will wake after ninety-five years, and he will be angry. I suggest that you tell him who really murdered the Light. He will be hungry when he wakes—he will need to feast. Perhaps send him one of the witch's henchmen." He says this last bit with a wicked smile on his face.

"I will definitely consider that, Michael." Lou peers at Clarissa's castle window and sees her staring out at him, angry and upset.

Michael looks in the same direction. "Ah. Looks as though you have your hands full, brother. Perhaps you can get your seer to cast a spell on that one to make her 'normal,' perhaps even human again."

Lou looks at Michael questionably. "If that were possible, and she were normal, would she love me like she did before?"

Gabriel interrupts. "Lou, you don't know what that would do to her, or to you. She could age like a normal human and die. You will need to ask yourself if you can handle watching the love of your life become fragile, Wither, and die."

Lou looks at her staring at him, her red hair flowing almost in slow motion. He notes on her beauty—and then the ugliness that she has become. It's as though she has become two people, one beautiful and the other haggard, green, wicked, and twisted. EVIL!

Lou's vision is interrupted by Michael's hand on his shoulder. "Lou, I believe it would be the right thing to do for you. It would give your heart peace, and it would dispel the evil within her." He pauses a moment upon seeing the look on Gabriel's face. "But that is only my opinion, brother. Ultimately it is up to you."

Lou holds the clock in his hands, realizing he holds great power. His life is changed forever because of the evil within his wife—his beautiful, red-haired beauty, his lovely Clarissa. *Her mother is to blame for all of this evil. If only he knew how ...* He sighs heavily, tears in his eyes. He looks at both of his brothers and then at his other much younger brothers around his castle and the mausoleum. "Thank you. thank you all," he says, clearing his throat.

Gabriel sees that it has been four Earth days since the lullaby. "We must go now, brother. You have many things to do. You have many things to explain to your citizens and decisions to make as well. Peace be with you." He reaches his hand out to put it on to Lou's shoulder.

Michael does the same. "Peace be with you, brother. Should you need us, just call us to be by your side."

Swiftly Gabriel and Michael extend their beautiful white wings and fly toward the heavens Gracefully, as do Lou's twenty-four younger brothers. Watching this exodus of his family is saddening. He turns around, seeing his son compelled to stone. *His family is murdered senselessly, and my beautiful Clarissa is a murderer. And for what? A future She ... argh.* Lou shakes his head and makes his way to the tower with the clock.

Madrid walks back into the mausoleum to make sure that she is able to turn James and Celeste into stone as well. It works, and they will stand the test of time. Now James will always see how beautiful and lovely his family was, even in death. He will never forget his son's face. As she walks back out of the mausoleum, she closes the doors behind her. She moves past James's great presence, shaking her head. She walks around him, looking him over, and then walks down the steps to the courtyard and toward the castle. Knowing that their world has changed forever, Madrid walks back toward the castle and to her room.

Lou walks to the highest steeple, places the clock in it, and fixes it in the corner of the room on a wooden table that catches some of the sun during the early morning hours of the day. After placing the clock on the table, he moves some of the other books and ink urns around to make sure that the clock will not be disturbed, moved, or stand out to catch anyone's attention. Once this is done, Lou turns, walks out the room, and locks the door.

After leaving the tower, he feels the overwhelming urge to see his wife. He walks down the long hall, passing the pictures of his father, his various brothers, and then the picture of him and an early picture of his family: him, Clarissa, and a young James. James was so young and happy. The picture almost brings him to tears.

Lou enters Clarissa's room and sits down. She is furious, crying hysterically. "What did you do?" she screams while kneeling in front of him.

"What needed to be done, for the future and for our son, and for our son's children," he says as he holds her hands.

"What does this mean for us, for everyone? For James?" she asks, grasping his hands tightly while tears stream down her face. She is frightened.

"It means that our son will be committed to stone for almost one hundred years, and nothing is going to change. We are all trapped in time, almost frozen, until James's true love is born again."

"What? You damned us to live like a stagnating pond of water?" she says, frustrated.

"No. We will only age one day for every ten, but we will have to acclimate ourselves to what is going on around us."

"I don't know how this is going to affect us, Lou."

He stands up because he sees that Clarissa is trying to manipulate him, putting both of his hands through his hair. Frustrated, he walks away from her. "I love you. I have *always* loved you. I have so many things I have to think about." Tears well in his eyes as he walks toward the door. He stops for a moment and turns around. Then he storms back up to her, grabbing her face with both hands and kissing her deeply. He runs his hands through her long red hair, holding her head to his face while his other arm wraps around her waist. He holds her body into his, holding desperately onto this moment, desperate to breathe all his love into her.

She releases herself from him, at once feeling guarded. Then she melts into him and kisses him back deeply, reminding him why he loves her. Tears fill her eyes, and they seem Genuine and full of feeling. Lou wants to believe that they are genuine. They run off her face and onto his as they kiss. He kisses her more, picking her up in his arms, and she squeals in laughter that he hasn't heard in many years. He pauses to allow the sunlight to catch her beautiful flowing hair.

"Oh, you truly are my beautiful baby!" he says. A large smile appears on his face. She smiles back at him as she finally knocks down the walls that they have built between them.

He walks slowly as he kisses her full red lips and lays her in the middle of the bed. Lou lays on top of his beautiful wife while they smile and kiss each other, stripping each other's clothes off piece by piece. He gets to her brassier and sees her shoulders. He stops. seeing how her long curls gently caress her smooth, warmly colored skin. He leans down and kisses her shoulder, and then he slowly licks and kisses her skin all the way up her neck to her face. He stops to look deeply into her beautiful hazel eyes. "I love you with all that I am. I love you, Clarissa."

She sees and feels his love so deep for her. "I love you, Lou. I love you!" Tears well up in her eyes as she leans up to kiss him. He meets her halfway, and they kiss so deeply that the birds around the castle seem to get louder, singing their praises of love. It has been so long since anyone has heard the birds chirp, let alone sing!

Chapter 8

It is morning, and James wakes to the present ...

James wakes to holding me, my long blonde hair catching the morning sun. I smile as I detects that his breathing has changed and he is watching me sleep.

"Y' know, a girl can get used to all this attention." I smile with my eyes still closed, and the sun carefully highlights my smallest of features.

James pulls me into his body. "I can't ever let you go. I love you. I love our babies. I love everything about you."

I feel that something is different in his voice. His emotions? Perhaps it is the slight crack in his voice. I turn my body around and peer into to those beautiful eyes. "Baby, I love you. You will keep me safe. You will keep our babies safe. I will not leave your side. I will listen to what you wish me to do, and I will do it."

He's looking at me with that "I want to believe you" look suddenly, I feel like I have to give him the pep talk.

I get up and straddle him like a pony. I feel both of his immense girths between my legs and under my now wet pussy, and I smile a minute. "Um, honey, I thought that ... well, both of those weren't prominent unless you were in your Guardian form."

He smiles up at me. "Oh, no! I figured that the cat's out of the bag, and you know about them. It's really difficult to hide one from you, so it's way more comfortable out. Know what I mean?" He shifts my weight and my body to a more comfortable position on them.

"Okay, getting back on track then. I think you need a pep talk."

"I do?"

"Yes, you do!"

"Oh, well, pep me up then, baby."

I smile while on top of him ok and say, "Look, you are a mean, kick-ass Guardian, right?"

Calmly he says, "Right."

"No! You're a kick-ass Guardian, and you don't take shit from anyone! Right?"

He finally has an epiphany as to where I am going with this. "Right! I don't take shit from anyone!" He gets that grin on his face and shows his gorgeous teeth. Mmm, I love that!

I start to bounce on top of him, getting a little excited. He starts to grow some fangs for me. I get more excited, and he senses that my pheromones are starting to kick in, so his eyes turn black. I get even more excited and shriek, "That's it, baby! That's my badass, sexy gargoyle Guardian, going to go out and kick anyone and everyone's ass! That's right!" I go to dismount him, and he pulls me on top of him again.

"Where do you think you're going, sexy mama?" he says through his fangs.

I give a bad-girl smirk and a sexy smile. I lick his lower lip with my tongue. He smiles at me with those gorgeous fangs, and I start kissing him deeply. He holds me onto him, kissing me and invading my mouth with his tongue. I feel he is fully erect between my legs. He immediately lifts me up and buries deeply within me. I am riding his thick girth as he thrusts into me.

I am riding and screaming, "Oh my God!"

He yells, "I'm cumming, baby!"

"Cum for me! Cum in me! Claim me! I belong to you!" I say as I look down at him with such love and lust.

I can feel him cum deep inside of me as he immediately lifts me up off of his cock and turns me around for doggie style. He's off the bed and thrusts his other cock deep into me. "Oh yeah. Fuck me! Fuck me, baby! Fuck it like you own it, Daddy!"

He pounds me harder, growling behind me, holding hard onto my hips, pulling me onto him hard, making me a part of him. I can feel my pussy wrapping around his large cock. I'm so turned on right now that my nipples are erect, and I am dripping from my pussy onto the bed.

He reaches for my nipples and begins to pinch them. Then he grabs them hard. I let out a whimper, and it only fuels his desire for me.

He pounds into my body hard and fast. My man lets out that roar that I have been so eager to hear, making my hair stand on end, my skin prickle, and my back arch in the pleasure that I have in fact pleased him yet again.

Ha! I think to myself. It isn't me this time who is slithering off his body and onto the bed, but quite the other way around. I smile to myself.

He slides out of my body slowly, and gingerly. Then he makes his way to the bed and lies down, exhausted. He sees me smiling down at him as I slowly crawl up to him, like a cat does when it is about to pounce on its prey. His eyes open a little wider. He smiles at me and then pulls the pillow around his face. He looks at me again with those beautiful teeth and that gorgeous grin. After catching his breath, he looks at me about to pounce on an exhausted prey, smiling with that naughty girl look on my face. He says, "Am I to guess that my beautiful baby did not get enough?" He quickly grabs me into his strong arms. I let out a squeak and then a giggle as he rolls with me, wrapping his body up with mine. "Didn't get enough of me, eh?" he says, almost breathless again as we both laugh and kiss.

I look up into those gorgeous, loving eyes. I reach up and touch his face, and even though his eyes aren't brown and golden at this moment, I can still see how much he absolutely loves and adores me. I speak with all of my heart so that he can feel it. "I will never, ever get enough of you, James!" I lean in to kiss him, and he has already met me to kiss me.

We lay there for a moment, and just then I feel it. "Oh my God!"

"What?"

"Did you feel that?"

"That? Where?"

"Here!" I place his hand on my belly.

"Whoa!" He is shocked and excited, and he smiles at me, pushing me back slowly to get a better look.

I lay back on my back, and James is quickly in on his knees, investigating this new Movement, however slight. "Oh, baby! They're beautiful!"

"You can *see* them?" I say, looking at him a little perplexed …

"Yes, just a little gargoyle heat signature image. It's my thing," he says as he looks up at me, smiling.

I look at him and return the smile. "What do they look like? Are they healthy? Are they beautiful? Do they have all ten fingers and toes?" Worried tears start to well.

James seeing how this is starting to affect me. He leans up and kisses me. "I love you. They are truly beautiful. They look like you. they are very healthy." He starts to well up a little while looking at me.

I say, "What, baby? Tell me …"

"I love you. Thank you for loving me and wanting to be my wife and have our babies, even knowing what I am."

I run my fingers through his hair and look at him intently. "Hey!" I lift his head, getting his full attention. "I fell in love with you. You, James. Your quirks, your imperfections, the way you love me. I fell in love with *you*, the whole package. And so it happens to be a Gargoyle with magical powers. So what? You're strong. Your parents are …" I pause to look around the room. "They've got a lot of money, and you've got major perkie poos. Like two penises! Um, yeah, like that is a real downer!" I say sarcastically.

He picks up his head and begins to smile at me being my normal, sarcastic, funny self. "Oh, and I get to be your wife, just yours. And I get to have your babies!" I lean in to kiss his nose. "Nothing is going to ruin that—I won't let it. I am pretty bad-ass myself when I want to be, and nothing is going to get at these babies. I promise you …" I get quiet and slightly serious, deeply looking him in those gorgeous eyes, into his soul. "I love you, James!"

He leans up and puts his hand on my belly. "You know, I am pretty happy that they look like you! I mean, what chance would they have in life if they look like me?" he says with a chuckle as he leans in to kiss me.

I interrupt our kiss. "About as much chance as getting their mother, eh?"

James pauses for a moment and looks at me. "Ah. Perhaps they will have their mother's brains too!" He kisses me long and hard. We lay in each other's arms and drift off for a small nap before going downstairs for a late breakfast.

James lies there holding me, remembering the dream he awoken from earlier, his past. He closes his eyes, holding me close to him. He wonders whether he be able to stop whatever may be coming for his family again … or whether he destined to repeat the past. He buries his nose in my hair. smelling my hair—that all-too-familiar scent that brought him to me again in the first place.

Chapter 9

I wake up and climb out of bed, leaving James asleep. I walk downstairs and hear Madrid and Lou talking in the kitchen. I stand within a few feet of the kitchen and hear Madrid.

"I dreamt our past last night, all the way down to when I turned James into stone."

"I dreamt too. That is why I have changed my mind about Clarissa being behind any of what is to come!"

"I am unsure. I am almost confused—it is as though our past has come to remind us of who we are, lest we forget."

I turn to look out the kitchen window at the newly fallen snow. The flakes are still shimmering down from the sky, kissed from the sun. Lou turns to Madrid. "Ever since that child has come into this house, it has been nothing but warnings from everywhere—but my Clarissa. I know she has changed from that day over a hundred years ago. I just know it in my heart." He clenches his fist and puts it to his chest.

"I can perhaps make her human, so that she cannot hurt anyone or anything," Madrid offers.

"But I can't live with the thought of watching the woman I love die."

Madrid drinks her tea and looks up at Lou with an epiphany. "Perhaps it can be temporary, just until the children are born and she sees that nothing bad is going to happen."

Lou stands and begins to pace the kitchen. His thoughts begin to come in almost panicked, fragmented waves. "Perhaps you have something ... we have to locate her. I don't understand where the hell she is! It's like she disappeared before she knew I was looking for her. This is so unlike her! I am thinking someone else is doing this, or pulling the strings. After dreaming about our past together, our sincerity, the way she ..." He pauses, thinking about how she looked at him, kissed him, told him she loved him. It was all truthful. "She loves me! I know she is not behind this. I just need to find her."

Just then James comes up from behind me, wraps his arms around me, and whispers in my ear. "You know, beautiful, it's not polite to eavesdrop."

I feel extremely busted. I whisper, "I just thought they were talking about me. I wanted to know if they liked me or not."

He picks me up, cradles me, and carries me into the kitchen. "So how did everyone sleep last night? Everyone like their trip down memory lane? I honestly thought mine was pretty shitty." He looks at Madrid and Lou. "Well? Anyone else like theirs?"

Madrid looks at Lou and then at James while steeping her teabag. "I have mixed feelings about mine, James."

"Father?"

"Argh ..." He sighs heavily. "Well, it was no rerun of *The Brady Bunch*" He pulls out a chair to sit down.

James says, "Well, my little beauty here was listening in."

Lou smiled. "Yes, I know. I can smell her pheromones. I smelled them just as she descended from the stairwell."

I try to defend myself. "I just wanted to know if anyone liked me."

Lou sips at his coffee. "Oh my dear, we have all been waiting for you for a very long time, and we are so very happy you are with us."

James says, "Oh, before I forget. We felt the babies move this morning. I didn't tell my little peanut here yet." He lifts me closer to him, getting everyone's attention. "We are having a little boy and a little girl."

I am speechless as I just jump higher into his arms, wrapping my arms around his neck.

Lou gets up from his seat, pats James on his back, and smiles at his son so proudly. Madrid rises and puts her hand on my head and on James's heart.

We flash forward to a dark grey time, where all four of us are standing in the courtyard. The air is so thick that we can cut it with a knife. Celeste walks forward with Jacob. The air looks like ash as they pass through it to come forward to where we are standing.

Madrid, feeling protective now, Says, "Death, be gone with you!" She tries to wave them away.

Smiling and understanding. they both look at each other and then back at the four of us. "Oh Madrid, we are not here to harm anyone. We are here to warn you of the danger that awaits in the coming moons. The babes will be born in solstice. James, you must protect them. A deceiver is among you, and yes, it takes the form of a familiar."

James sets me down to me feet slowly and carefully, still keeping me close by his side. He is careful not to break our bond. "Did you make us all dream of the past last night, Celeste? Did you warn us about this?"

"No, my love." She shakes her blonde hair like he reminisced so many times before.

"It was me, Father." Smiling up at him is the tiny face of Jacob. It is the voice of the child James thought he would never hear, the child he thought he would never see.

"Why, my little child! Tell your father why." James smiles because his greatest fantasy has now been fulfilled.

"Because you all needed to be reminded of your sacrifices, of why you are here and what you are all fighting for. That is why," he says in his tiny voice, looking up at his father so proudly.

James looks at Celeste. "I loved you so much. I tried so hard, honey." Tears stream down his face.

"James, I love you. I never stopped. I am with you again. Our spirits are once again whole, but different. I am different this time than I was last time. You have me again. We must go now." She holds Jacob's hand, they begin to walk up the stairs. They are at the front of the mausoleum.

Just then, James lets go of the bond. the four of us outside in the snow, in front of the mausoleum. James opens the doors of the mausoleum and rushes in. Their bodies that were so carefully cast into stone all those years ago are now ash on the table. James places his hands into the ash, lifting up the piles of ash and running his hands through it, shocked. He looks back at Madrid. "How?"

Madrid is shocked herself, looking at Lou in disbelief. She shakes her head slowly. "I do not know."

I slowly walk up behind James. "They have gone to be with God."

It was an idea that no one had thought of, not even myself. It was something that occurred to me, and I said it as quickly as I thought it.

James turned to me. "You must be right. You *must* be." He picks me up in his arms. holding me tightly. "Honey, let's go. There's nothing here to see anymore. This has been a place of pain; I feel it. For some strange reason I don't know why, but I do."

I nod, grasp his hand, and lead him out.

Madrid and Lou stay behind.

Lou asks, "What happened here?" They stare at the table, both in disbelief.

"I do not know, my lord."

"I believe that when we find Clarissa, all things will become clear. Until then, these and other things are going to be a mystery." He turns his head to look at Madrid. "We must be very watchful from this point on. Things are not going to be as they seem."

"Yes. I will scry for Clarissa to see where she is, to bring her back to the castle."

"Good. I will hail the center to see if they have knowledge of her whereabouts."

Madrid turns to Lou. "My lord, every time you seek knowledge from that source, you fall. if you wish to rise to grace, your contacts with that source should remain scarce."

"I understand, Madrid, but something is obviously going on here, and if we don't find out what that is soon, history is going to repeat itself again. I don't believe we have another hundred years. Do you?"

Lou places both of his hands on his head in utter frustration, and he runs his fingers through his hair. Madrid watches him closely, waiting to see what he may want her to do next. He covers his eyes for a moment with the palms of his hands, sighing. He runs his fingers through his hair completely and then looks at Madrid with watery eyes. "Okay, there is nothing left to see here. Let us go now."

They walk out of the darkened mausoleum and into the cold winter air, making their way back into the castle.

The ash sitting on the table slowly lifts off the table as though a breeze has taken it, swirling the ash into long, thin tornadoes in the cold winter snow. It disappears into the ground, into oblivion. "Ashes to ashes. As it once was, it must be," a whisper in the wind chants. Then there is quiet once more.

The stillness is almost frightening to the earth, and the ground begins to tremor slightly.

Back in the castle, glass begins to shake, almost like a full-blown earthquake. Some pictures that hung on the walls are shaken off their nails and drop to the floor.

"Madrid!" Everyone is frightened and looks to her for a supernatural explanation. The tremors last but a mere moment. and then they are gone. Nothing is broken, but everyone is a bit shaken.

Lou asks Madrid, "What just happened?"

"I am not sure. but whatever it is, it must have something to do with the very strange events of today."

James attempts to change the tone of the room. "I don't know about anyone else, but I am starving, and I can hear Charity's stomach too. Why don't we go get something to eat? Maybe then we can all look at things with clearer heads."

I reach for James's hand. He takes it and smiles at me, pulling me into him as we depart for the kitchen. We enter the kitchen, and James opens the refrigerator door pulls all sorts of food out, stacking it up on the counter. Lou starts to laugh to himself as he sits in the chair at the table. Madrid starts making sandwiches for everyone. James is extremely hungry, as is Lou.

Lou interrupts the different conversations going on at the table with one I hadn't thought of. "Charity, have you thought about getting your apartment closed up and moving completely in with James, now that you two are engaged?"

I pause because the thought hadn't occurred to me until this moment. Everything has been moving so quickly. "Honestly, I haven't thought about anything since I left for James's place. Everything has been moving so fast," I say awkwardly as I start picking the bread from my sandwich into tiny little pieces and putting them into my mouth.

"Oh my dear, I didn't mean to make you feel rushed. I just thought that James' brothers could help move you completely into his home while you two stay here. That way you wouldn't have to worry about anything. I will take care of everything."

"I wouldn't want you to go out of your way ... And brothers?" I looking quickly at James for an explanation.

Lou claps his hands together and laughs. "Oh my dear, he has many brothers! James is the baby!" He laughs to himself as he gets up and kisses James in the middle of his forehead. James continues to eat. "So I will take that as a yes, then?" Lou smiles.

I just can't tell him no. "All right, but I would love to meet James's older brothers, if it's okay with you."

Lou kisses me on the top of my head. "Of course it is, my dear girl. Of course it is! I will call them right away! We will have you moved quickly, and everything will be perfect, I assure you."

I knew that this had to be true. I trust him; this is my family now. I look at the man I love shoveling food into his hungry mouth. Madrid is starved as well, and Lou accepts me and wants me as a part of the family, smiling at him. I say, "Thank you. Thank you so much for everything."

Lou looks at Madrid and says, "I'm going to contact a few of James's brothers now. I'll be back in a few."

James finishes eating and says, "I'll go with you, Father. I want to know who is going to be there." He quickly leaps over to me, kisses me, touches my face, and says, "I'll be back, beautiful. I love you."

I smile at him and kiss his beautiful lips. "I love you too." I watch as he leaves the kitchen with his father.

Madrid smiles very big and asks in her very distinct, almost Jamaican accent, "So, how did you two meet, my girl? I know the first story, you see, but I don't know this one." She reaches to touch my hand, and she holds it. I smile. "Oh, don't fret none, baby. It helps me see what you see, and I even see the things that you don't see … even the things in the darkness."

"Okay." I feel a little weird, but I'm okay with it. I'm not sure where to start, exactly."

"Well, start at the beginning, with your ex-husband. It's always good to start at the beginning."

"Okay, but that wasn't very pretty."

"The past isn't always pretty, my dear. That is why we cleans our souls, to make room for something better, something right, something that is meant to be."

I feel that I can talk about it with her and close my eyes. I think of a place to begin to talk about Tino. "Okay. I think I have found my place."

Madrid has the ability to see every word I say as though she is living the words, my life. It's as though she has been there.

I met Tino through a mutual friend. I had graduated college and had been a crisis intervention specialist for Butler for only six months when my girlfriend said that she had a friend who picked me out of her high school photo album.

I had gone to her house for a party, and it was crowded. There were a lot of people, and he was playing DJ. He was attractive, I have to admit, but I really wasn't looking for a relationship. I could see by the slurring of his speech that he was already trashed. At this time my girlfriend came up to me and said, "So, what do you think?"

"Of …?"

"Tino! Isn't he gorgeous?"

"I don't have an opinion. He's trashed already," I said, looking at her and peering at him over at him uncomfortably. "And by the way, what did you mean when you said he picked me out of a photo album?"

She sucked her straw full of sex on the beach, almost drinking her glass completely dry, and then she put her arm around me, slurring her words in my ear. "He said, 'I need a nice, good girl, honey. One who is gonna love me. So I took out my photo album and gave him a bunch of pictures, and I started turning pages. He stopped dead on you. Even before I could give him any other pictures to look at, he wanted you!"

"Really?" I say, looking at him pessimistically across the room. "What does he do?"

"He's, um …" She giggled to herself, and then she fell over on her butt, still laughing. I attempted to pick her up. she pulls me to the floor with her. "Shh!" she said, laughing and splattering spittle as I wiped the side of my face.

I asked again. "Honey. what does he do? Does he have a job? Does he work, live at home with Mommy and Daddy? What?"

"He's a paperboy!" She slides backward, still laughing hysterically.

"Nice … okay." I got up and turned around, and I see Tino in the flesh—and in my face. He backed me up against the wall and had my hair in his hands. His face was deep in my neck, smelling me. Admittedly, it gave me a tingle. I went to push him away from me nicely. but he grabbed me, pushed me backward, and kissed me hard. For some reason, I kissed him back. Maybe it was because I was secretly lonely or heartbroken. Or maybe it was because dealing with people with crises of their own reminded me of just how messed up my own life was, and I just wanted to be with anyone at this point, maybe even a pushy drunk.

I got called out for a crisis call one night, and Tino was happy about it because we were arguing over some woman that I had caught him with. He had her in his car and was holding her hand. He said he wasn't, but I walked up on his side of the car and had full view of the interior of the car. When we got home that night, all we did was argue. I was also happy to get that call, to head out and actually help someone with a problem. I drove out to an area unknown to me in East Butler. I had to park three blocks away, and it was just beginning to storm. I grabbed my bag with my crisis paperwork and headed out.

I walked up to the house and assessed this couple who had the same problem that I had been dealing with right before I'd left Tino. I felt a huge lump in my throat. The husband kept insisting that the wife was crazy. I took the wife into the other room and spoke to her privately with a police officer. She was adamant and said that she even had pictures on her phone of the husband and the mistress. The police officer went out and asked for the wife's phone. The husband was reluctant to give it up, and so the other officer told the wife to come out and get it. We all viewed what she was talking about, and The husband was arrested for falsifying information and for attempting to have his wife involuntarily committed. The wife was so upset. I couldn't blame her!

I had been there for about two hours with that whole fiasco. I felt somewhat vindicated and believed that I had done something good for someone else. I began to make my way to my car in the pouring rain.

"Argh! I hate thunder and lightning!" I muttered to myself. I made my way down the street and said hello as I passed a man on the street. At that moment, I was quickly shoved into the alley. I screamed! The man fought me for my purse, and I finally ended up giving it to him because he punched me in my face, knocking me backward into a puddle.

That night I do remember meeting a nice guy, though I could never remember who it was. It continued to rain hard. I was on the ground, crying hard. I remember sitting in that alley wondering, *Why me? Why me, Lord? I've been a good girl. I help lots of people find their way back to you all the time. I feel lost, and now this?* I cried in the dark. Then this man came out of nowhere, helped me to my feet, handed me my purse, and said, "Don't cry, beautiful." He lifted me almost on his own without any power from me. He held me up as I stood there, mascara running down my face, my tears still streaming. "You know, you're even more beautiful when you cry. Do you know that?"

"I don't think so." I couldn't see through the mascara burning my eyes and the pouring rain. I kept trying to wipe my tears and mascara in order to see who this man was. He said I was beautiful! "Thank you. thank you for getting my purse back. I don't have much money."

He smiled with the most beautiful smile. He took my breath away. He chuckled as he came close to me—close enough that I thought he would kiss me. Instead, he touched my long, wet, blonde curls, smelling me and taking me into him softly, slowly. "Let me walk you to your car, beautiful."

He held me up and helped me walk almost blindly in the rain. I noticed that he was strong, muscular, and kind of large, but I was fighting hard to see well enough through the pouring rain. I asked. "By the way, what or where did you find my purse?"

He gave that gorgeous smile. "From the man who took it," he said candidly.

I paused as my brain tried to process everything that had happened today: Work, the crisis intervention, my robbery, and now this. I was being walked back to my car by Mr. Gorgeous!

We got to my car; the walk was over, sadly. My hero had to say good-bye, and I was sad. I didn't want to say good-bye. I looked up at him. "Thank you so much for helping me. I mean it, really."

"It was no problem at all. Well, be safe. You need to get home, get warmed up."

"Yeah, I do. I have to be at work again in the morning."

"And you may want to put some ice on that lip of yours," he said as he touched my lip gently.

I winced in pain. but I hadn't given it much thought of it since he had come to my rescue. My strange, dark hero. "Um, yeah. I had better take care of that too." *Wow,* I thought to myself, *I could take care of him!*

He smiled too, almost like he knew what I was thinking. I had the keys in my car door now. I opened my door, and he helped me in. He looked at me as I wound down my window and closed my door. "Now, you get home, gorgeous, and maybe I'll see you again."

My mascara had to be running down to my chin by now. "Oh God, I hope so. Thank you for everything! I would have been lost without everything in my purse."

"Go ahead, get home." He waved and began to jog up the street to a car parked near mine. I never saw his eyes, just that beautifully sculpted jaw line and that gorgeous smile.

After getting into his Camaro, he turned the key, and Skillet's "Feels Like a Monster" blared from his car stereo.

"Mmm, awesome song!" I muttered to myself as I turned the key to my own car. I thought of him all the way home, almost in a daze.

Then it occurred to me about three-quarters of the way home. What happened to the guy who grabbed my purse and shoved me in a puddle, and why didn't my hero take that hoodie at least partially off of his head to show me the rest of his face? Was he horribly scarred or something?

During the trip home I was in a daze, and now my lip and jaw were beginning to throb. I walked in the door, and Tino was standing there waiting for me. "What the fuck happened to you?" he said in a snide tone.

"I was walking back to my car after my crisis call, and I was mugged. I fought back," I said with a prideful tone in my voice, carrying my lip like a badge of honor.

"Looks like you got your ass kicked," he said, laughing as he headed back to the bedroom, smoking his cigarette. "Next time. maybe you'll learn to give them what they want, and maybe you won't get fucked up!" He laughed one last time as he closed the door behind him.

I sobbed quietly to myself, took the ice out of the freezer, and wrapped it into a towel to place it on my lip. I sat in my spot on the couch in the living room, placing my pillow on my lap and crying quietly to myself. I could hear Tino laughing at the television in the background, like nothing had happened. He had no pity, no sympathy.

I heard something outside. I was not sure what it is—a growl like a dog? I went outside to investigate, but the sound had stopped, much like the rain. I went back inside to my spot.

The following month, I have to admit I went back to East Butler to see if I could bump into my hero, but he was nowhere to be found. I simply thought I was lucky once to have had him that night. God had had him there to serve one purpose, and he had.

I hadn't been feeling too well, so I made an appointment with my doctor. She ran some tests and said that I was pregnant. The news was mixed for me. I came home and told Tino; he appeared to be happy. I honestly thought that this was a new beginning for us. I was always and forever hopeful.

Two weeks later, I began to have pain in my abdomen, and I couldn't get comfortable. I couldn't sit, stand, or lie down. Nothing I did made it any better. I called the OB/GYN, and they brought me in immediately. They did an ultrasound and found that the baby was a little over three months but in my fallopian tube. It had a heartbeat, and every time he moved. he caused me pain. They needed to go in immediately and remove the pregnancy.

I called Tino. We rushed me up to the hospital, and I saw the woman who was in the car with him that day. She was a nurse! Oh my God! All I kept thinking about was, *My baby has to die so that I can live. My husband's mistress works in this hospital.* My head was beginning to spin at a hundred miles per hour. The nurse came into the room with five surgical papers for me to sign, stating that the baby would be buried with all the other babies that were "terminated." That word ate me alive. I wasn't terminating my baby—I wanted my baby! I began to softly sob.

Tino stood in the corner of the room. He walked over to me and got my attention. I looked up at him, thinking he was going to say something comforting to me. He said. "If you don't stop this fucking crying shit, I'm fucking leaving your ass here!"

I was in shock, and tears continued to roll down my face. I had an ache in my heart so very deep. These people were making me choose the life of my baby or mine, and this man, who swore to God that he would love me for better or worse, just said this to me? I finished signing my papers. I lied back on the bed, rolled over, and quietly cried to myself. I couldn't look at him again. I knew in my heart that as soon as they wheeled me into surgery he was going to be right there with *her*. He wasn't going to give me another thought.

Right before they put me out, I begged them, "Please, could you move my baby where he belongs? Please don't kill my baby. He didn't do anything wrong. Please!"

I remember waking up alone, in a cold room. Tino was nowhere to be found. I was sure he was in the hospital—with her. But not here with me, where he should have been. I closed my eyes and wished for my hero to come rescue me from this heartache. No one should have to hurt this bad.

I went back to work the following week, and I caught Tino again with that slut. Finally it was over. I began looking into an apartment. I put enough money away for the first month and a security deposit. I would figure the rest out as I went. I waited until he went to work one day, and then I had movers meet me at the house. They moved all of my belongings out of the house quickly and across town within a few hours. We had everything set up, and I was in my new home and settled. I have to admit, I was very nervous, but I knew it would all be worthwhile.

Madrid sits there, hanging on my every word and smiling at me. I look at her and ask, "Are you okay? Do you want me to stop?"

"No, child. Continue. I love this story! I can't wait to see—I mean, hear some more!" She smiles at me, and I feel comfortable enough to continue on.

Okay, I moved out and left Tino a letter telling him that I had cleaned out our bank accounts, filed for divorce, and never wanted to see him again. I said he could have fun with his whore.

I didn't leave a forwarding address, so I was pretty confident that it would take him some time to find me. Still, I was pretty careful about being followed.

One day I was shopping at the Giant Eagle, getting some groceries to put into my new refrigerator. I bumped into this guy who was tall and really built. He had a hoodie on, and he smelled really, really good, but he had the hood up over his head. I couldn't see his face again. He smelled like Compelling cologne and car grease, but he wasn't wearing leather. He smiled at me again, and I sighed. I thought, *Again with the teeth! And that smile!* We both laughed.

This time I broke the awkward silence by saying, "You know, I don't have that fat lip anymore." I licked my lip. "See? Perfectly kissable." I slowly slid my tongue across my lower lip, feeling my heart beating faster and other body parts beginning to awaken down south. I looked intently at his mouth, wishing I could run my tongue across his perfect lips and just taste him.

I could see his mouth crack a smile. He started to bite the corner of his own lip, and I could see he was trying to contain himself—as was I.

Interrupting my fantasy, I quickly said, "Your meat is dripping." He was still standing there biting his lip, and watched as his tooth grazed his goatee mustache and that lip. He looked at me through the fabric of his hoodie. I touched his arm. "Hey, sexy, your meat is dripping all over the place." I picked it up slowly and placed it into his cart, smiling at him, feeling flirty and horny as hell. I knew that I had to do something to catch this gorgeous, sexy hero! I rifled through my purse, pulled out a piece of paper and a pen, and looked up at him. With a smile, He was still staring at me.

I wrote my name and address down on a piece of paper for him. While handing it to him, I said my name. "I'm Charity."

"James," he said in a caveman kind of way, beating his chest with his fist.

"I owe you dinner," I say, laughing at the way he said his name.

"You do?" he asked, clearing his throat and smiling.

I still felt flirty. "Yes, I do, and I won't take no for an answer." I had a glow I hadn't felt before.

He looked down at the piece of paper. "So, 7542 Melrose Lane? That's where you live? That's a nice little place." He grinned a little.

I nudged his arm a little. "Hey, I'm newly divorcing, and that is all I can get. Still, I can call it home. It's my little shelter, of sorts. There're no drive-by shootings, rapes, or burglaries—well, not yet this year. I'm doing good," I said, so proud of myself.

"You are too adorable, you know that? I am looking forward to dinner at your house at six o'clock tonight. I will bring the merlot."

I was so excited that I almost jumped. He smiled again.

I continued with my shopping, checked out of the store, and put all my bags into my car. I got home, took my bags into my apartment, and turned all my music up high. I was singing at the top of my lungs. Don't judge me. "Sing unto the Lord a happy tune," they say. They didn't say it had to be in tune!

I went about chopping the lettuce and the tomatoes, and shredding the right amount of cheese. I made everything look just right. I had a roast in the oven, and I made the gravy perfect, not that store-bought stuff. The potatoes were the real thing too; a man can tell the difference. I also made asparagus—I don't know why, but I thought he would like the complete meal.

The table was set. the candles were on the table, and my hair was in an up-do except for a sexy little curl I let down on my right side, and the little curls I let down by my ears. I had some cute little white rose earrings on, and my little black dress. Now I waited.

Outside, Madrid sees James comes to the door. He is dressed handsomely, but something is wrong. He comes around the side of the building, and she sees something. She sees him come out with Tino. She holds onto Charity's hand intently. She sees him pick him up by his throat, threatening him. "Do not ever come back here again, or I will kill you! Do you HEAR ME ASSHOLE?"

"That is my wife!" Tino says.

"You don't deserve her. She is *mine* now. You are a miserable fucking pig of a man who did nothing but mistreat an angel. She wanted nothing more than your love and respect and you cheated and shit all over her. Get the fuck out of here and never come here again, or I swear no one will be able to identify your remains!" James snarls closely in his face as his eyes change to black and his fangs protrude. "Oh, and you will sign the divorce papers tonight and mail them back, or I will find you—and that won't be pretty either! Do we understand each other?"

Tino asks, "Does this apply to all women?"

"Hell no, just with this one. You will leave this one alone. This beautiful goddess belongs to me, has *always* belonged to me. Go home, pig. Sign those papers now, and mail them back and free her from you! However, a word of caution. You never know when you may come across a mere man who may not take too kindly to the way you treat these women. You may not live to tell the tale!"

Tino runs to his car, parked a street down, and drives away. James watches and then leaves the street. James looks in the window to look at his blonde beauty checking the clock. It's now almost eight o'clock. "Shit! time flies when your kicking some dirt bag's ass!" Peering in through the window, Charity sitting there almost hopeful that she will have me for dinner, bursts into tears, quickly blows out the candles, and races down her hallway and disappears out of sight. "Oh baby," James mutters to himself. "I want you so bad, if you could only know. I have to call you and clear this up. I know how I am going to fix this. Pausing and muttering to himself, "Exactly how I'm going to fix this?" He looks around. "Now, where is her car? Ah, there it is!"

Madrid smiles and even slips out a small chuckle.

I say, "What?"

"I'm sorry, child. I didn't mean to interrupt you. You said James called you?"

"Yes. he said that he couldn't make it—some car trouble."

At that moment, it all became clear as day. I sat back and started putting the pieces together.

Madrid smiled at me, still holding my hand. "Take your time, child. It will come to you." She is nodding cautiously, smiling.

"Okay, so my hero who was at the right time, right place... James!"

My suicide attempt when I almost walked out in front of a speeding semi and was pulled back after losing my baby. I had no one to talk to, and a voice in the sunlight said, "Your life is far more important to me, and to God, for you to do this!" It was James! The figure looked like an angel, wings and all. I say, "I didn't tell anyone about that! Not even you, Madrid."

"You didn't have to, child—I saw the whole thing as I was holding your hand. I saw your whole life, my baby girl. All the pain, Hurt, loneliness. I saw how that bastard hurt you! He got what he deserved!"

"Did he see me cry? He *did* see me cry! He has been watching me. Oh my God, for years he's been protecting me! James! He couldn't have!" I look at Madrid.

"What, child?"

"My car."

Madrid holds my hand a little tighter now. "Sit down. I have so much to tell you. James, you, and your babies are all part of a bigger destiny. One thing you should know is that he has loved you your whole life. I remember one day he came home upset, over a little girl. He said, 'Madrid. they made so much fun of her for wearing glasses! It hurt her feelings.' I asked him who, and he just shrugged my question off, saying, 'Some cute little blonde girl I saw sitting alone in the play yard by herself.'

"Then you were talking about all those times with your husband. Well, I do remember those times as well. James came home, tearing through this house and furious with his father, screaming at him. 'She never would have met that asshole if you didn't make me go with you to Italy! Today she almost took her own life because of him! Her baby died, and he couldn't give a damn! He didn't care if anyone hurt her, or if she died! Just as long as it doesn't intrude on his bottom line or his time with his gutter slut!' Yes, my little one, he cried for you, shared in your grief. He wanted to run to you and hold you when you needed held, and he watched as you struggled with sneaking out of the house, moving while your husband was at work. He watched diligently that day, in the shadows. He wanted to make sure that you were going to be safe! So understand that every time you felt alone, you were never alone. Every time you felt like you didn't matter, you mattered the world to him. Every time you felt as though no one loved you, know that he loved you so much, he would have parted the Red Sea for you!"

I sit there listening to Madrid, trying to go through my memory banks. *Did I see James before, maybe in passing?*

Madrid says, "Ah, I see what you're doing. let me explain. We were all enchanted by the lullaby of time. We only age a day for every ten of your years. So does that explain the question that you have swimming around in your head?"

I think about all those times when I was growing up, and when my parents died. I remember there being a man. I close my eyes Briefly, trying to remember if it was James who held my hand. I was so young when they died, and I felt so alone. I am having an epiphany. I am smiling and then laughing. "Madrid, did he do something with my car the next day?"

"No. That night he caught Tino outside your apartment, and they got into a fight. Let's just say that James didn't want you to see him all sweaty and dirty. He wanted to make a good first impression, But he kept looking at you in the window, and he wanted you in the worst way!"

I nod and then laugh. "He kept his face hidden from me, even in the store. All I knew was his first name. And that gorgeous smile! He wanted me? Oh my God, I wanted him so badly." I bite my lip, thinking about the things I wanted to do with him after dinner.

Just then, the two angel men return. "What's going on in here? Is there a party, and we weren't invited?" James says loudly, laughing.

I quickly spring to my feet, tears streaming down my face. I kiss him deeply. "I love you, I love you, I love you. If I had known ... if I had known, honey, I would never had left."

"Whoa, baby! What's going on here?"

Madrid rises from her chair. "I asked her how you two met. I wanted to see, and so I held her hand. Before I knew it, she had it all figured out. All of it."

He smiles at me and holds me close. He can feel my heart pounding hard in my chest like it has never pounded before. "Honey, please calm down."

"You are who I have been waiting for my whole life. My whole life! I prayed and prayed, and it came to me in a dream. 'He will come to you.' You have been watching over me, protecting me, loving me for so long. You saw me cry and still thought I was beautiful."

"Oh baby, you remember that?"

"Oh yes! I couldn't get that out of my mind: your smile, and how you picked me up, touched my wet curl, and my swollen lip. You still thought I was beautiful."

"Dad, Madrid. we have a lot to talk about," James says, smiling with tears running down his face. Apparently he never thought that I would ever find out, ever put it together.

Lou and Madrid walk closer together in the kitchen, nodding. "Son, take the time you need. It will be done, as we discussed." Lou then waves us upstairs.

James picks me up and carries me upstairs, kissing my head. I say, "I love you, James. I love you. I know that you are my soul mate. I love you."

We make it back to our room, and James sets me down on my feet. I back him up against the wall and start kissing him like crazy, stripping off his clothes. I run my fingernails down his back, and it drives him wild. I rip my shirt off and take my ponytail out, letting my blonde hair fall down all over my shoulders. My breasts are fully exposed. He lets out a grunt and then a growl. I slam his body up against the wall and kiss him again. His fangs cut my lip slightly, and the taste of blood fills our mouths. I don't care. His tongue enters my mouth as I unbutton his belt and unzip his jeans.

I slide his jeans off, careful not to hurt both of his now hard cocks. I take off my sweatpants and then my panties. I am naked now, and I fall to my knees. I take turns sliding each cock into my mouth, sucking one and stroking the other, trying to find a rhythm. He is so fucking hot right now. He picks me up against the wall; slides one of his cocks into my hot, waiting pussy; and makes love to me. He is kissing me with more love than ever before. We have no more secrets.

He holds me up and lets out his wings, and then he changes into his full gargoyle form. Now he can be himself. "Oh yeah, baby. I love you, only you, all of you!" His tail turns me around slowly around my waist, and his wings make a slight bed for me to lay on my belly as he slides both of his cocks up my ass and my pussy. He begins to pound me hard and fast. I am loving all of it. "Harder! Faster! Oh my God, I'm cumming!" I look back, and he has this look on his face that he is so satisfied and proud. I begin to squirt all over him, and then he cums up my ass and my pussy at the same time. He lets out a shriek, and as he cums deep inside of me, he pulls me into him and steps backward, holding me carefully as we go toward the bed.

We end up on the bed, and James is almost in his human form except for his tail, fangs, and eyes. His tail is still wrapped around my leg. I turn around and curl into his body for the warmth. His tail grabs onto the blanket, pulling it up toward his hand. He reaches for it and pulls it up over us. He kisses my forehead and then my face. I move my face back and kiss his lips.

"I finally belong. I finally belong," I say.

"Baby, you've been saying that since you were six years old, that you didn't belong here."

"How long have you been watching me?"

"Your whole life. I would have stepped in at the right time before Tino, but I had to go to Italy for my father for a month. When I came back, you had already met that asshole, and there was nothing I could do but stand back and watch. So many times I wanted to …"

I say, "I wished someone would have."

"My breaking point was when you walked out in front of that truck, after he said that shit to you before you had the surgery … after the baby."

"You have to believe, I couldn't make a decision like that. I begged them to save him, and they killed my baby anyway. A part of me died with him, and after I woke up alone, I didn't even think God was with me."

"I know that you didn't know it, but I was there with you. I was with you the whole time, beautiful. And after that assbag said that rotten shit to you, I desperately wanted to rip out his throat. But I knew one thing: one day soon. you would be mine, and I would show you what true love would feel like. You'd know what it feels like to be desired, wanted, needed, and most of all loved every day."

"James, I love you. I am so sorry I ever doubted you."

"Let's not think so much about the past, but focus on the future. We need to be married Soon, and these babies of ours are going to need all of our love," he says as he squeezes me close to him, kissing me on my head. "Oh, before I forget, my brothers are going to have your apartment emptied out by tomorrow night, and everything will be integrated into my—I mean, our house nicely. There won't be any worries." He looks toward the ceiling, almost concerned.

"Are you sure that it won't be an inconvenience?" I say, worried myself.

"Nah." Clearly he's lying to save my feelings. James gets this horrific picture in his mind of his brothers. Although they are harmless, they're the biggest perverts he knows. Little do I know it, but they are probably dancing around with my underwear on their heads right now. He tries to get that picture out of his mind before it's burned in there for all eternity. He finally says, "We're engaged, so we need to be married before these babies come, honey."

I'm a bit shocked while lying in his arms. I lean up, moving my long hair out of my face to look at him. "I think a spring wedding would be nice, and I can wear a nice gown that's big enough that I won't look like a mutant marshmallow walking down the aisle to say our vows," I say with some nervous apprehension.

James laughs. "Marshmallow? I like marshmallows. Yummy! I love mutant marshmallows even more!" He says this as I begin to whine a little bit, and he pulls me into his warm body. "Baby, you are the only one I love, the mother of my children. I have loved you forever, and besides…" He leaves a long pause. I look up at him, waiting for the next words. "I love me some mutant marshmallows!"

I get up and hit him with my pillow. He laughs as he grabs me and pulls me into him. "Oh baby, I love you! So, spring? You'll be gorgeous! I will tell Father and Madrid that our wedding will be in the spring. Madrid and Edgar can help with the preparations. I assume that you will want your girlfriend to be your maid of honor?"

"Oh my gosh! Yes, honey! I have to call her. Ever since I took leave from my job, I haven't had a chance to talk to her or anything!"

"Well, perhaps when the weather breaks, we'll go home—our home—for a weekend. You and she can go for coffee and cocoa." He pats my belly. "The doctor will be here in a few days to check on you, so let's get some rest."

Chapter 10

At the table, Madrid and Lou talk about the doctor coming in the next few days to finish bringing the final pieces of equipment to monitor the pregnancy, as well as the labor and delivery.

"So that room is just about finished?" Lou asks.

"Yes. He is bringing the ultrasound equipment tomorrow, and we will begin interviewing the people who will attend to the doctor during his visits and the birth."

"I trust that you will handle that task?"

"I have no problem with that, my lord. There have been more than enough strange things going on the last few months that have raised even my eyebrows, and I want to know who will be in this house."

Lou smiles at Madrid and then sighs heavily, as though the weight of the world is upon him. "What troubles you, my lord?"

"I must go and meet with the unmentionable one …"

Madrid is shocked and immediately concerned. "My lord, I thought that perhaps you may have changed your mind."

"Madrid," He starts, looking at her worriedly, "I want my Clarissa! I want my family back together!"

She sees the look of despair wearing him down, as though he has not been sleeping well. "Okay, but if you are going to be with Evil, please take something with you to protect you, so that you won't fall." She looks at him worriedly and almost pleadingly.

"Okay, Madrid, if it pleases you and you will leave me to my business. I will take whatever it is so that you will let me go, but you must make haste because I must not be late. This entity does not take well to tardiness."

Madrid runs off and quickly grabs at her dress and apron, yelling behind her. "You will be safe, my master. Yes, you will!" She turns the corner of the castle, heading toward her quarters and leaving Lou far behind her. She runs into her room and finds an ancient Native American medicine bag. She searches through all her herbs on her shelves and finds the right combination: basil, fennel, rosewicket, anise, wormwood, and dragon's blood.

She begins burning the dragon's blood, going around the room clockwise and smokaying the entire area. She places a pinch of fiery wall of protection powder in the four corners of the room. On her altar she grabs her box of graveyard dirt in a glass, and then she carves the word "Protection" into one of her white candles using a coffin nail. She takes the liquid from the glass and wets the length of the candle. Then she places her St. Michael medal next to the candle.

Madrid lifts her hands up to the ceiling. In a loud, commanding voice she says, "Protect him. Protect Lou with your fiery sword, Michael." She then lights the candle and takes four blue candles, carving the names of the four archangels into each one: Michael, Raphael, Uriel, Gabriel. she wets the length of each of them with the water from the glass. After taking the candles, she places them to represent north, south, east, and west, placing them respectively on the altar. She begins to light each one, chanting loudly. "Michael. Michael, burning bright. Protect Lou now, with all your strength!" She moves to the next. "Raphael. Raphael, burning bright. Protect Lou now, with all your strength!" She burns the third candle. "Uriel. Uriel, burning bright. Protect Lou now, with all your strength!" She then burns the last candle. "Gabriel. Gabriel, burning bright. Protect Lou now, with all your strength!"

She surrounds the white candle in the middle of the altar. Madrid takes a piece of old scroll paper, an ink well, and a pen. She writes the name of the evil that Lou will be encountering three times: "Annanuki, Annanuki, Annanuki." She burns the scroll in the middle of the candles and gathers the ashes. Then she places it in the medicine bag with the spices and races down the hall to Lou.

"My lord! Here, wear this. under your clothes. I must go to a crossroads as you leave, but if you leave now, I will take care of the rest!"

Lou puts the medicine bag over his head and places it under his clothes, looking at her, perplexed. "Madrid, what have you done? Will I be detected?"

"No, my lord. Now, go! Do not be late, or he may suspect something is amiss." Madrid adjusts his shirt and his coat. She peers out the side of the door; the snow is still falling. She quickly opens the door without a word and ushers him out.

Lou walks out the door and down the stairs to Edgar, waiting in the Limousine to take him to see the Ancient One.

Madrid races up the stairs to James and Charity's room, and she knocks on the door quickly.

Startled, I jump, and James gets to his feet and runs to the door, opening it quickly. "Madrid, what's wrong? Are you okay?"

"James, I cannot drive, and I need you to take me to a crossroads right now. I must bury this into the ground now."

"Okay, let me get dressed. I will be down quickly."

Madrid immediately turns around and departs for the stairs, not saying a word. She knows that James will be down behind her within moments.

I look at James running around and getting his shirt on. "Can I come too?"

"Um, well, yeah. I think it's about time that you see a little bit of what goes on around here. Dress Warm, baby. Hurry."

I rush to my feet and quickly throw on my sweatpants and a sweatshirt. I pull my long blonde hair out of the neckline of the sweatshirt, and as I look up, I notice that James is staring at me with that grin that says, "You are so damn adorable!" It's these moments that make me love him so much.

I smile up at him. "Hey, sexy, are we ready?"

He takes his hand and wipes his moustache and beard, revealing a beautiful smile. "Yes, beautiful. Let's go. I've never kept her waiting before—she's probably already on her way back up the stairs."

We walk down the stairs, and Madrid is waiting in the hall. We walk to the rear of the castle, a part of this large place that I have never seen before. We walk briskly behind Madrid, and I glance at many portraits—almost frightening ones that almost tell a story of a war. A war in heaven?

We turn a corner in the hall, and the portraits are interrupted by a large door. James opens the door. There is a large set of white and grey marble stairs leading down. James turns on the switch to the right and looks back at me while Madrid descends. "Are you all right?"

I smile but hold my belly. "Yes …"

He quickly grasps my hand. "Come with us. I know we must make it to our crossroads soon, so we have to get to a vehicle."

I place my hand in his. without hesitation he picks me up in his arms. His wings extend out of his back, and his eyes change. He is holding me a little tighter as we begin to fly down the long stairwell.

Madrid is already at the bottom, waiting. We land softly, and James kisses my lips gently as he puts me on my feet, touching my belly with his hand.

He moves over and looks for the light switch on the wall to the left of where we are standing. The lights illuminate the largest garage I have ever seen! "There has to be at least twenty vehicles in here!" I note.

He picks the key of the car he wants, and Madrid breaks the silence. "Well, I should have known. Of course he would pick that one! Come, child. Let's walk over there. it's that black one with the blue on it."

James says, "Oh Madrid, How can you say that about a Chevy SS Coupe?"

Madrid and I look at each other. Boys and their toys. We roll our eyes.

James is motioning for us to get to his muscle car. "C'mon, ladies. I thought we needed to get there Quickly?"

We quickly rush to get into the car. I get in behind James, and Madrid takes the passenger seat. The front doors close almost simultaneously. James looks in the visor and sees the garage door opener; he pushes the clutch in with his left foot and turns the key. He puts the shifter in second gear and slowly lifts his foot off the clutch petal. The car begins to move, and I get excited as the roar of the engine begins to throttle beneath us.

We are outside of the garage now, and the snow is no longer falling. James touches the garage door opener again, and the door begins to close behind us. I am watching him as he shifts between gears, pushing the clutch petal again and now moving the shifter into third gear now, then fourth and fifth. We are trying to get Madrid to her destination, a crossroads.

Within minutes Madrid breaks the silence, pointing to a break in the trees. "There! There, James!"

James drives his car through the snow, almost spinning out through the tree line. He pushes the clutch pedal again, then the break. This time he pumps the brake, careful not to spin the car uncontrolled in the snow. He puts the car into neutral and pulls up the parking brake.

James jumps out of the car, looks into the back seat, and says to me, "Stay inside the car. You can look, but stay inside. Okay?"

Madrid goes out to where she needs to be. James opens up the trunk and pulls out a shovel. I look at him perplexed. almost worried.

He runs over to Madrid. He looks at my face and smiles a little, almost letting out a bit of a chuckle before he starts digging a hole for Madrid to place her candles to protect Lou. He looks up for only a moment at Madrid and says, "You know, she's probably in that car saying, 'What the hell are they doing? Digging up dead bodies or something?'"

Madrid laughs and then says, "That's deep enough." She quickly takes the satchel and places it into the hole that James has dug. James begins to fill the hole quickly, and after he fills the hole, he lifts the last shovel of dirt up to Madrid. She takes a handful, standing on the pile and holding her hands up waist high. She begins to let the dirt sift through her fingers as she turns around in a circle, and then she stops. She says nothing until she stops and puts her hands together in a praying motion, looking up. "Protect him. Please protect him. In the name of love, please protect him."

James walks back to the car, puts the shovel back into the trunk, and closes it. He gets into the driver's seat, closes his door, looks back at me, and smiles. "Are you okay, beautiful?"

I smile at him with that confused, "unsure what to ask first" look. I clear my throat. "Um, find anything interesting out there?"

James smiles, shifting himself in his seat to look at me better. "What you saw was Madrid finishing a spell."

Madrid gets in and looks at the two of us. We can go now."

James smiles at Madrid. "Oh, by the way, our wedding will be in the spring." He is still smiling at Madrid.

She turns to him, her thick accent rolling off her tongue, not amused. "Don't you dare use that boyish charm with me, child! That might have worked with your mother, but your mother is not here now!"

These two obviously now how to work each other. They begin to stare each other down, but he is still smiling ear to ear. I start to hold my baby belly. Madrid has a lock on his face with her eyes; this is almost like a contest. These two are almost nose and nose, and my heart begins to pound. It is dead silent in the car, except for my intense breathing.

Suddenly Madrid raises her hands. "All right, then! Of course there's gonna be a wedding! You know, I was going to plan the wedding for you, child! Happy now? Now we can go!" She smiles back at me. My heart is still pounding. "You okay, child?"

All I can do at this point is nod. Words escape me.

James looks at me in the rearview mirror, smiling. Maybe I am just not feeling well.

Lou arrives at the Ancient One's dwelling. He exits the limousine and walks through the front doors. There are very large security men there who wand down Lou and send him onward to the waiting Ancient One. There sitting in a large chair looking at swimming koi is an elderly Chinese man. The room has a very deep, ethnic Oriental feel.

"I see that you are feeling a little Chinese this time, Old One."

The man grins, leaning back into his high-backed chair and folding his long, fingered hands, which are almost decrepit with long, wicked fingernails. "So, Lou. What is it that I may do for you?"

"I want to thank you for seeing me, but I am sure you already know that I am desperate to find my wife, Clarissa."

"Yes, yes ... I may have heard that she disappeared. But I need to assure you that the demons and the Annanuki have had nothing to do with the disappearance of your lovely witch. However, I do believe that perhaps you should look a little closer to your lineage for the answers you desperately seek."

Silence fills the air as the Ancient One rises eerily from his chair. He almost floats across to the pond, where the koi are swimming around among the many different rocks and tiny mountains and waterfalls. He motions for Lou to come to him, and Lou quickly rises to follow. They stand at the side of the water. The Ancient One stands there for a moment, closes his eyes, and then speaks. "Lou, can you hear the peace that the water gives the koi?"

Lou closes his eyes, and listens to the water for a moment. He hears the water falling and then splashing upon the water below. The koi are sliding upon one another. "Yes, I do."

"Fragile is this planet, and the life upon it."

The Ancient One pats Lou on his arm and then walks toward his chair to sit down. "For instance, you, my boy, are eternal. However, your witch is not, and yet you seek her because she completes your existence."

Lou sits down in the chair across from the Ancient One.

"This planet with its myriad of seasons, years, centuries, life, and most of all feelings amazes me so much. With every form I choose to take,

I learn a new perspective on thinking, believing, and respect for many things."

Lou looks at the Ancient One respectfully as the being extends his hand to Lou. Lou gives his hand to the Ancient One. "Ah, I see James is fulfilling his destiny Wonderfully, but it is not your wife that impedes his destiny. It was and is closer than you think. Oh, there are two children this time around? How beautiful and fragile life is. You must be so proud of your James!"

Lou smiles. "Yes, I am. Since he has awakened, he has been watching her, taking care of her. He has chased that human garbage away for good—without killing him." Lou smiles to himself for a moment and then continues. "Charity is growing those babies wonderfully, and James is growing stronger every day ... and more attached."

The Ancient One smiles, showing razor sharp teeth as he leans back into his chair. "Ah, so she has taken to his Guardian form as well!" He laughs eerily. "That is all wonderful, Lou. Now, I will put some pressure to assist in the search for your wife."

Lou leans into the desk that separates the two of them. "Ancient One, I thank you humbly for your assistance. What may I offer you in return?" He is a little frightened but humble.

The older being smiles again. "I only ask one simple thing. I ask that when you get an ultrasound of the children, I receive a picture of the children as well."

Perplexed, Lou says, "A picture, Ancient One?"

"Yes. While the children are still in her womb." He smiles.

Lou says happily, "Yes, Ancient One. I do not believe that will be a problem. I have made all the arrangements for the doctor to do all of her care at my home, to keep her safe because Clarissa disappeared." He pauses and sighs.

"Oh Lou, the heart is such a fragile device, is it not?" He looks around the room with the black satin walls and many other Chinese water features, unfolding his hands and waving slowly in either direction. "I have become many different nationalities and individuals over the centuries, and I have come to realize that love, fear, hope, and despair are some of the strongest emotions that a body can handle. Happiness is fleeting; it lasts only as long as it is able to, and then it is gone. I can say that I sympathize with you, Lou. I have also felt love."

He touches the pad attached to his telephone, and a sound comes over the speaker. The Ancient One begins to speak in his language. It is made up of some soft clicks, shrill shrieks, and a long, hiss. The Ancient One's eyes go from being human to a shiny emerald black. Then he touches the pad again, and his eyes turn back to a light brown to match the elderly Chinese man he has decided to portray. He clears his throats and begins to speak again. "Lou, I have just added much pressure to find your beloved Clarissa, so if all goes well, you will have her back soon. Now, if you excuse me, I have to take my leave and address some issues that have come to my attention."

Lou stands and bows to the Ancient One, who returns the gesture. Lou lifts his head to rise, and the Ancient One is gone.

Lou looks around the room and sees that he is truly alone. The doors behind him open, and security says, "This way, sir."

Lou takes his coat and puts it on as he walk out the doors. He heads out the main doors and out into the weather to his waiting limousine. He quickly gets into the car and shuts the door. Lou knocks on the glass between the front and rear and says, "Home." He then sits in the back of the car. alone with his thoughts, reminiscing of his Clarissa.

He remembers their first, real kiss. He can almost taste her sweet lips as he closes his eyes, flashing back many years ago. Her long, red flowing locks; running through the fields of honeysuckle and flowers; her tripping and her laugh ... he smiled to himself, nearly landing purposely upon her. "Oh dearest Clarissa, how beautiful thou are!"

"My king, you flatter me! You can have any fair maiden, yet ye set chase to me!" she says with a lovely smile upon her face, looking up into his eyes.

"I love you. Marry me and be my wife. I cannot live one more day, one more cold night, one more loveless century without your love, Clarissa."

The sun is bright. Lou's memory is interrupted by a car horn beeping. He shifts his position in his seat, and the limousine begins to move again after the abrupt stop. He thinks about her soft, full lips. He closes his eyes again, sighing deeply. He can almost smell the scent of her beautiful, soft skin. The way she looked at him was like no other! While peering up to the sky, he folds his hands together and begins to pray. "Father, I know that I have fallen from your graces, but please. I have done so many things to make things right. Please, I beg of you. Please give me back my Clarissa. Lead her back home to me. I promise to continue to do right by you. Please."

Tears stream down his face. The ache in his heart is so great that he promises to himself he will never share his heart or his bed with another, ever again, lest it be with his beautiful Clarissa.

I have not been feeling well since we got back from the crossroads. I am starting to feel cold inside—really cold. My appointment with Dr. Seoul isn't until tomorrow, but I feel crappy now. I lay in the bed, and James comes upstairs to see how I was feeling.

"How's my little patient?" he says nervously.

"Cold. I can't get warm."

"Okay, Well, maybe we need to call Dr. Seoul."

"Okay."

He's shocked that I don't resist. He kisses me on my forehead and says, "Okay, baby, I'll contact him, and then I'll be back up and will keep you warm."

"Okay."

James races down the stairs without hesitation, and Lou and Madrid are in the kitchen. James says to Madrid, "We have to call Dr. Seoul. Charity is upstairs, sick, and she never asks to go to the doctors." He looks worried.

Madrid immediately picks up the telephone and calls Dr. Seoul. "Doctor, yes, can you come? Yes, she is not well. Immediately. Thank you, see you then." She hangs the phone up and turns around, "The doctor will be here within the hour. Maybe she needs something to drink."

I am suffering quietly. afraid to allow anyone to know, afraid for there to be a repeat of Tino. I pray for the pain to subside ...

I begin to have some cramps in my belly, and I start to cry. "Oh God, please. No! I beg of you, please. Please don't take another baby away from me. I can't take it!" The cramps seem to worsen, and now I begin to scream uncontrollably. The pain is sharp and like a rake deep within my body.

Deep within my womb, Aniah, the female of the twins, can't regulate her own body temperature. She is beginning to weaken and wither. James Jr., the male of the twins, senses he is losing his twin. He mutates into a tiny gargoyle, rips open his placenta, tears into Aniah's placenta and enters hers, and pulls his placenta behind him with his tail quickly so Aniah doesn't lose any amniotic fluid. He leans up against the tears that he had made, building his body heat and stopping the liquid from leaking out. The spontaneous labor slows and then finally stops. James Jr. swims over in his gargoyle form, wraps himself around Aniah, and begins to warm her. bringing her body temperature back up to a normal range. A warm glow surrounds them as Aniah and James Jr. heal their placenta's as the two are now joined within the walls of one placenta.

James hears my screams and races through the hall and up the stairs, almost ripping the door down to get to me. He sees me screaming on the bed with my legs spread, my back up against the headboard. My hair is wet as I reach for him. He gently crawls on the bed to be with me.

"James! James, Oh my God, Oh My God! James, the babies, the babies James, something is wrong!" I'm terrified and unable to breathe through the pain, grasping his hand tightly. I look at him. "Please, honey. Please make it stop!"

Everyone comes running to me. I'm in a deep sweat. The bed is wet, and tears are streaming down my face.

Then without warning, the pain just stops. James and Lou looks within my womb to see what has been happening, and they see something strange.

James looks at Lou questionably. Lou motions for James to go out of the room after they get me calmed down and comfortable.

Madrid and Edgar change the sheets. James picks me up. I'm worn out, Sweaty, exhausted.

I look up at James while he holds me. "She was cold."

While waiting until Edgar and Madrid remake the bed, he holds me closer.

"Aniah ... she was cold, so Junior saved her." I lick my lips, parched from all the screaming and sweating.

James looking over at Lou, worried and concerned. Everyone hears what I say. Lou nods.

James lays me down gently into the bed, kissing me on my forehead, cheeks, and then my lips. He kisses me on my belly and whispers, "Good job, boy!"

Everyone but Madrid leaves the room. Edgar continues down the stairs with the sheets. Lou and James stand outside the door. Lou puts his hand on James shoulder. "I need you to breathe. She will be fine. Junior saw there was a problem, and he handled it." He can't help but smile. "He *really* handled it!"

"Dad, what the hell! This is not funny! This is hard on her! Is she going to survive this birth, having these babies?" James is worried and angry.

"I can't answer that. There has never been twins like this before."

"Like what before?"

"Mono babies, or mono twins."

"What?" James is shocked because he has never heard of such a thing.

"Mono twins, usually same-sex twins, share the same DNA and placenta, and sometimes one of the babies doesn't survive. Our problem is that he has just entered her placenta, with Aniah—did Charity just say the child's name? Hmm ... Anyway, this event has never happened before. Twins of opposite sexes must have their own placentas. Your son felt that Aniah was in danger so he destroyed his own to save her." Lou stands stoic and a flash of worry crosses his face. "So, we have a problem."

James is shocked for many reasons and says, "I think I need to sit, have a drink, or maybe both."

Lou pats him on his large shoulders. "The only thing you need to know is that Charity is going to be just fine, as are your children."

"No, that wasn't it."

"Then what is the problem, son?"

"I don't know what is more disturbing: the fact that you knew what had happened and that you were freaked out like I was, or that you knew what all those medical terms were!"

"Oh. son! You can't live a few hundred centuries without picking a few things up, can you? All I can say is that I've used my time wisely down here. Now, go be with your wife."

James walks back into the bedroom. looking at me lying on the bed, my hair now soaked with sweat and tears. I'm exhausted. He lies down next to me. "How are you feeling, baby?"

I barely open my eyes. "A little better. But I have to tell you, if that was an indication of what labor is going to be like, I want drugs!" I say with as much humor as I can possibly muster.

He pulls me into him, laughing a little as he slides down, kissing my head and hugging me tightly. He seems worried not for what is out there to get me, but what is in me, that he put there.

Madrid is still sitting on the side of the bed. She hears voices coming up the stairs. "Oh, the doctor is here!"

Walking into the room is Edgar, Lou, Dr. Seoul, and the doctor's nurse. Seoul puts his bag on one of the chairs in the room, pulls out his stethoscope and carefully wraps it around his neck, and hands a few other instruments to his nurse. He walks over to my side of the bed. "Charity, I see that you have had a rough couple of hours." He begins to listen to my heartbeat. James moves away so that he is not in the way of the doctor.

"Abbie, hand me that device." Seoul reaches for a small boxlike radio with a microphone on the end of it. okay "This is going to let us hear what is going on inside your belly, little one. Okay?"

He turns on the machine, and at first no one hears anything but static. He puts a little cold gel on my belly and then places the microphone on my belly and begins to roll it around. At first we hear two heart beats, and then the machine is ripped out of Dr. Seoul's hand, flies clear across the room, and lands on the floor! I lay there, watching the whole thing happen, but I'm too exhausted to care.

Everyone in the room gasps.

They all start to mouth the words to each other, "Did you?" they all shake their heads.

Dr. Seoul smiles and says, "Oh, that must have just been a bit too slippery. Slipped right out of my hand, it did! Abbie, will you be a dear and pick it up? Wipe it off and take my bag and things down to the car for me."

"Yes, Dr. Seoul." She runs over, picks up the sonar device, wipes it down, shuts it off, and puts it in his bag. She leaves the room with Edgar as her escort.

Dr. Seoul picks up my wrist. "How are you feeling, Charity?" He's a bit worried.

"Tired, like I need to sleep for a couple of days."

Just then a tiny voice, Aniah, says, *We just want to go to sleep, Mommy.*

I look at James. "Aniah says, 'We just want to go to sleep.' So do I, baby. Can I just go to sleep?" I am trying to keep my eyes open but am finding it harder and harder to do so.

Dr. Seoul smiles and pats me gently on my shoulder as he rises to his feet. Madrid follows him to the hallway, as does James.

Lou is waiting for everyone to meet him outside in the hallway. Finally, James comes out and gently closes the door.

Lou breaks the silence. "Junior has entered Aniah's placenta to save her, and possibly to save himself."

Dr. Seoul crosses his arms. "Obviously the little ones saw there was a serious problem to their mortality and did something about it."

James smiles. "I'm proud of my children, but at what cost is this to Charity?" He is almost gritting his teeth.

Madrid quietly listens as the men converse about the current situation. "Well, I believe that there needs to be an ultrasound done, to make sure that they are both moving along as they should," she says intently, putting her hand on James.

Lou interrupts the discussion, clapping his hands. "Well, okay then!" He points at James. "You. Go in and be with your wife. Now." James walks back into the bedroom, closing the door behind him. "Doc, Can you come back in a few days? Give her the weekend to recover from ... whatever happened here." He points to Madrid. "Madrid, can you make her something supercharged to eat and drink, to deal with the enormous changes going on within her body?"

Madrid bows her head and closes her eyes. "Yes, my lord. I will tomorrow. Let the child sleep tonight." Madrid departs for the stairs.

Dr. Seoul waits until he and Lou are alone in the hallway. "Charity has connected with these babies as they have connected to her. She can *hear* them telepathically."

Lou stands there surprised but not alarmed. "Are you saying the Charity is taking on *powers* of telekinesis as well?"

"I'm saying that she doesn't leave this house to have these babies, her life and the lives of the children will be in jeopardy. I believe that there will be many new surprises awaiting us and Charity's new gifts."

The two depart for the stairs and go their separate ways.

James lays with me, taking my slowly drying hair into his fingers. He tells me how much he loves me. He leans in to kiss her my head, Whispering, "I love you so much, sweetheart."

James gets up and turns on the small lamp in the corner of the bedroom, just in case I may need to get up in the middle of the night. He then walks over and turns off the large overhead bedroom light. After sitting on the edge of the bed, he takes off his black boots and jeans. Finally he takes off his white T-shirt, leaving on his boxer shorts and socks. He climbs under the blankets, sliding his body all the way up to me. I open my eyes slightly. James kisses my lips slowly and lays there holding me.

Sunlight comes through the windows, and James is awake and still watching me sleep. James slides out of the bed and goes into the bathroom. He walks out and sees that I am still sleeping, undisturbed. He puts on his jeans, a pair of slippers, and a clean T-shirt. He runs down the stairs to the kitchen to make a pot of coffee and breakfast.

Madrid wakes to hear all the noise in the kitchen. She grabs her robe and a pair of slippers and leaves her bedroom to see what all the commotion is. She turns the corner and sees James racing around in the kitchen, trying to make breakfast as quickly as possible. "Child! What are you doing!" she says with her hair tussled, uncombed, and not up in her gele as it usually is when she is ready for the day.

James is startled; he's not used to seeing Madrid without her hair put up. He stops and smiles.

Madrid touches her black hair and smiles herself. "What you *doin'*, child?"

"Um, I'm trying to make Charity breakfast. She needs her strength. She's still sleeping, and that's not like her."

"I will make her some things to eat. Take her up what you have made here, and I will make her some things after this." She points to the mess he has made in the kitchen. "Everything will be just fine. You need to have faith, boy!" She walks back toward her bedroom.

James finishes putting everything on a tray: coffee for him and Charity, eggs, and toast. He climbs up the stairs to their bedroom.

James opens the bedroom door and sees me getting up. My belly looks three times bigger than it was the day before. "Whoa," he says under his breath. putting the tray of food down.

I get up to my feet and stumble to the bathroom and to the toilet. "Wow, baby! Oh my God, I lost my feet!"

He stands in the doorway, sympathizing with me. He's smiling and wiping his face like he always does when he is stressed. "Baby, you are beautiful ... gorgeous."

I stop him. I cautiously wipe myself after going to the bathroom and slide my panties back up. Then I waddle to the sink to wash my hands. James comes up behind me, wraps his hands around my huge belly, tucks his head in my neck, and kisses up my neck to my cheek, making me laugh.

"You are beautiful, gorgeous. You're the mother of my children, and I love you endlessly!" He stares back at me in the mirror as he wraps his hands cautiously around my belly, holding my hands over my T-shirt.

I sigh, thinking to myself and feeling a bit nostalgic, even emotional. *Yes, I think to myself, this is another one of those moments. The ones you breathe in and want to touch, feel, and experience over and over again. This moment is bliss ...*

There's a knock on our bedroom door as Madrid enters with a tray of food. "This is for you child. You must eat and keep your strength up."

Walking over to the two of us as James helps me back into bed, she appears to be somewhat shocked at the size of my belly. Madrid places the tray on the bed and touches my belly. Looking up amazed, she smiles at me. "You eat child. Eat, it will nourish all of you." Madrid departs, leaving me and James alone.

"I was pretty scared for you yesterday."

"I was just as scared honey, but I feel confident that everything is going to be all right now."

The day went on as James helped me get a shower. What better way to conserve water than to shower together? He made sure the water was exactly as I love it to be, hot but not scalding. Standing there waiting for me in his sexy nakedness, made me excited to get a shower.

I walk to him as he stands there in the bathroom with the water running. He wraps his arms around me as he kisses me deeply. I look up into his eyes, "I love you."

"Oh baby, I love you."

James steps into the shower as he reaches out his hand to help me in. I take his hand and I step in.

The water is hot as I put my head back, letting the water penetrate my hair. James pulls me into him, kissing me hard. His hands slide through my long wet hair. I can feel his girth rubbing on my belly. He reaches for my soap sponge and my Caress soap. Placing the soap back on the shelf, he begins to lather my body. I press my lathered breasts up against his chest, transferring soap onto his chest. I run my hands slowly through the soap and his chest hair. I look up into his eyes with that sly smile. "Make me your naughty girl." I whisper to him as he leans down to soap my ass.

I reach down and begin to stroke his long thick shaft. I feel him sigh. It has been a long time since we made love for fear we may hurt the babies. I reach over to the shelf behind James and grab my Wen shampoo. I pump a sizable amount into my hand and begin to work it through my hair. James lathers my breasts over and over again as I finish rinsing my hair. I giggle as his hands are all over my body. I love that he makes me feel sexy and desired. We finish up in the shower as James steps out, once again lending his hand to help me out of a wet shower. He begins to dry me off. He takes his time drying my breasts and my ass as he gently dabs my belly dry with the towel. I begin to walk toward the bed, turning my head winking at him as I leave the bathroom.

James dries himself quickly with the towel and walks quickly to join me. I am lying on the bed with the sheet up over my breasts. He comes to the my side of the bed, leaning down kissing me as he slowly slides the sheet off of my body.

"Are you sure?" James says concerned.

"We are alright now, yes honey, make love to me."

His eyes light up with delight as he slowly climbs onto the bed hovering himself over me. He slides his thick girth into me as I quickly moan and arch my back. He sees how I react as he starts to gently slide back and forth into me trying to not hurt me or the babies. I kiss him deeply as I tell him, "My turn."

He quickly but gently complies. I carefully mount his rock hard girth and ride him until I cum. He hold on to my waist as I continue to ride him until finally he roars. I can feel him explode deep inside of me. I lean down, pressing my belly into him, kissing him slowly and passionately and dismount him. We lay on our bed holding each other through the night.

I wake the next day to Madrid knocking on our bedroom door, and she then enters.

James looks up at her as she stands over him. "Come now, Charity must wake to let the doctor examine her."

James takes his hand and rubs my thigh to wake me.

"I know, honey. I heard her," I say, somewhat grumpy because I hate being made to leave this warm bed.

James slides his legs out of the bed, resting on the edge of it momentarily. Madrid sees that we are waking, and so she leaves.

"C'mon, baby. we are going to see the babies on the ultrasound shortly," he says, clearly hoping that this prospect might make me move a little quicker.

"Grrr!" I growl as I move my side of the blanket off of me and slide myself to the edge of the bed. James comes over to my side of the bed to see if I may need assistance getting to my feet. I take his hands as he helps me to my feet. We both quietly shuffle sheepishly to the bathroom. We exit within minutes of each other and begin to dress. James is very awake, but it takes me a little longer to gather my senses.

"Are we ready?" he says as he slides on his shoes.

"Yes, let me just get my slippers on."

We depart the bedroom and head down the stairs. James doesn't leave my side, helping to make sure I'm not dizzy and won't fall down the stairs.

We approach the room they have been working so hard to put together for the babies' birth. James opens the door, and Dr. Seoul is there with a different nurse.

Seoul walks toward me. "Welcome, Charity. Here, please put this gown on and then get up on the bed." The nurse smiles and exits the room with Dr. Seoul.

James also gives me a huge grin. I am overwhelmed by that beautiful smile and his gorgeous teeth. His smile is so contagious that I have no choice but to smile too. He is overly excited, as am I. I get my gown on with James helping me to take my clothes off. He helps me up onto the exam table, but after looking at this thing, it is more similar to a bed.

James kisses me on my head as I lie down. The doctor and his nurse walk back into the room. I smile at the nurse as she gives me a warm blanket. "What's your name?" I ask.

"Oh. I'm sorry, Charity. My name is Samantha. I'm Dr. Seoul's nurse today."

"Nice to meet you."

James is in his own world as he looks at everything that Dr. Seoul is doing. Samantha hands Dr. Seoul the ultrasound gel, and he squirts it on my belly.

"Eek! That's cold."

James smiles at me, growing with excitement.

Dr. Seoul puts the ultrasound ball on my belly. He begins to smile as he turns the monitor toward us so we can see the picture that is forming. "Well, we know what happened the other night."

James scoots his chair closer to my bed, looking intently at the monitor. "Okay, What *did* happen, Doc?"

Seoul points at the monitor as he freezes the frame. "If you look here, it looks as though they are sharing the same placenta. Here is James Jr.'s, and it is tucked behind the growing, thriving one. He is still connected to it, but he is now in Aniah." He continues to roll the ultrasound around my belly. "All in all, they're healthy and growing. Aniah is a bit smaller than I would like, but I'm sure she will grow."

Dr. Seoul continues to take freeze frames. He then hits a key on the machine, and it begins to print. He tears it off, looks it over, and then hands it to James and me.

James smiles as tears fill his eyes. "Oh, baby! Junior is hugging Aniah, and they're holding hands! This is so beautiful!" He immediately rises to his feet to kiss my lips and then my face. Dr. Seoul prints off additional pictures and clips them to the inside of a chart.

I look at these pictures of two precious babies growing inside of me, and I start to tear up. James kisses me. "I love you, Charity! Thank you, baby! Thank you for loving me!"

I place my hands on either side of his perfect face. "I couldn't love anyone else but you. It's always been you. I love you, James."

Samantha wipes my belly with a warm washcloth and then dries it. Okay. Seoul begins to do an internal exam. I feel uncomfortable. He finishes, and it can't be soon enough.

"Okay then, everything looks good. I see some blood from the event the other day, but there's no reason for me to believe that it won't dissolve. Your womb replaces the amniotic fluid every four hours or so and your body will absorb the blood that is outside your womb. You can get dressed now."

I say, "Wow, so the babies look okay I don't understand how Junior can be in the same placenta."

Dr. Seoul Is trying to figure it out. "I don't think I know myself," he says as he walks toward the door with Samantha. "Go ahead and get dressed, and we'll schedule another appointment."

Dr. Seoul walks out and is received by Lou, who says, "Well?"

"She and both of the babies are just fine. However, the babies are now sharing the same placenta."

Lou looks questionably at the doctor. "So do you have any idea what any of this means?"

"I am not sure. But I will say they are healthy." He takes out the pictures of the babies and hands the ultrasound to Lou. Lou looks down at the picture. "Thank you doc. I know someone who is very interested in this pregnancy."

Lou looks at Dr. Seoul. "May I keep these pictures?"

okay "Surely."

"Thank you."

Dr. Seoul walks toward the front door with Samantha. Lou walks them out and says, "We'll see you soon."

Lou closes the door and walks to his office. He reaches for an envelope and writes on a piece of desktop stationary. There is a gold engraved "A" with a red border surrounding it.

> Annanuki,
>
> Here are the pictures of the babies, as promised.
>
> Lou

Lou walks out to the hall, sees Edgar, and hands him the letter. "Please mail this immediately."

Edgar, not known for his talkative nature, nods. He walks toward the kitchen and puts on his coat and hat as he exits the kitchen door.

A week later.

The Annanuki is given the letter from a Chinese woman wearing traditional garb. He nods and smiles at her as she exits the room, closing both his office doors behind her.

After opening this envelope, Annanuki begins to smile with razor sharp teeth. "Ah ha! Charity is one of mine! Now I'm confident that the babies are a blend of all, and will be powerful." He leans back into his chair, looking down at the photo again. "Mono babies … all three belong to me. They all have quite the destiny to fulfill now."

Chapter 11

Spring

Winter's harsh hold has finally lost its grasp on the world. The grass is starting to turn green, and the trees are showing the first new birth of spring. I'm beginning to waddle like a duck. This pregnancy has been anything but normal.

Jeannie is here, and we are working out the final plans for this wedding. James and Lou have been searching for a straight nine months now. Our wedding is going to be here in no time, and James's mom won't be here. I can feel his pain. As a matter of fact, I can feel all sorts of things. I can feel empathy for everything—or as Madrid says, I was always empathic, but since I've become pregnant those senses have only grown stronger. I know things just by touch, or by dreaming. I've seen my parents in dreams. I now know I have never truly been alone.

Jeannie and I are paging through the flower displays and other last-minute things. The wedding will be small. Jeannie is excited because we are sitting on the couch in the great room, and she is so happy for me. "I can't believe it, Miss 'I'm never going to let anyone get close to me again' is getting married—and having babies!" She reaches over and rubs my belly. The babies love their Aunt Jeannie; I can feel them adoring and loving her as much as I do.

Jeannie and I decide on which bouquets that we like, one for each of us. For me, calla lily for me and red roses with baby's breath and some white and red carnations mixed with long greens. Madrid's and Jeannie's bouquets are just as beautiful, only a little smaller: red roses and white and red carnations. I simply love them.

I am getting excited because the wedding will be in the next four weeks. I feel as big as a house. Dr. Seoul said that I may go a month overdue because they're twins, and these are my first full-term babies.

"Jeannie, I hate to say this, but I think I need to lie down for a little while. Do you mind?" I ask.

"Weirdo! Go lie down. You have two gorgeous babies sucking the energy outta ya! Go take a nap; I'll be here when you wake up."

I give her a quick hug and walk slowly out of the great room and to the stairs. I take my time climbing each and every one. "Finally!" I say to myself. I'm here, and now it's time for a nap. I lay my hands on my belly, and I can hear and feel the babies laughing. This fills me with so much joy! My best friend in the whole wide world, my babies finally growing in my belly, and the man I love. For once in my life, I can finally close my eyes, drift off to sleep, and know that I am safe. James will keep me and everyone safe.

I never had that with Tino; I always felt anxious, scared, alone, and afraid to do anything wrong that might piss him off. He would verbally assault me until I couldn't speak anymore. I remember so many nights when I went to bed, crying softly to myself …

I crawl into bed and close my eyes. I wake up two hours later. I wonder if Jeannie is still here or did she get bored and go home. I run into the bathroom to pee. I quickly flush, wash my hands and take my time down the stairs. I make it to the great room and find her sitting, reading through the bridal book. I sit down next to her. "How was your nap rip van Charity." She says jokingly.

"Long." I reply smiling back at her. I pause thinking about my safety and how James and his family make me feel safe and secure. Jeannie detects that my mind has wandered.

Jeannie touches my arm. "What's up, honey? What's on your mind?"

I smile a little, and then tears start to form. I just can't stop them. "I don't know. I was sitting here thinking about how happy I am now, and then I started thinking about all those horrible, hurtful things Tino would say to me. Now I'm crying!" I say.

Jeannie holds me close to her. I can feel the warmth of her body leaning into mine. "I can tell you're really happy now, sweetie, but you have to learn to let go of those people who poison your spirit and hide you away from everyone by telling you that no one wants to be around you. You have such a beautiful life now, right here with James."

I nod and wipe my eyes with my sleeves. "Yeah, you're right. I guess that I was thinking about things that will and probably never happen."

Perplexed, Jeannie pulls her back away for a moment. "okay, like what?"

"Like Tino should feel bad about all those things he did to me, said to me—you know, not ever being a husband but more of a roommate. I was there to cook, clean, fix his medication, and all those convenient things. But never was I important to him. Why? I just want to know why couldn't he be in love with me? Why was everyone else so damn important?"

Jeannie now understands that this is closure that I am asking for. It's one thing to pack your things and leave, get divorced, and then nothing. "Honey, he was a pig. He always had to be smarter, better, faster at all things. But you went to school for your degrees, and he had a whole new thing to be insecure about. Because you are smarter than he is, by many different levels. He was afraid you would make more money than he would, be completely independent of him, and he just couldn't do that. You always had to be his lesser, not his equal."

Her words speak to me like a love song. "Yes, you're right. He isn't worth my tears, my frustration. I mean, James is so wonderful to me. He takes his time with me when we make love, not just climbing on and climbing off that quick." We start laughing.

James walks into the great room and says, "Is there a party going on in here?" He has on his blue denim jeans. His beautifully sculpted body matches his gorgeous facial features. He walks straight up to me, kneels down in front of me, kisses me, And then starts talking to the babies.

I have to lean back because they get excited! "Whoa! Wow, they love their daddy!"

He places his head for a moment on my belly, and then something happens. A flow of knowledge comes to me almost instantly!

I sit there for a moment, and then I speak. "The Guardians, created before Christ, before man. God's most challenging warriors." Within a few fleeting moments, it is as though all the knowledge of how the Guardians came to be is downloaded into my brain.

They were the perfect match for the archangels. God created one angel at first, his most beloved. The Light was his first, and God was most proud. The Light reminded God that this child was of his very own hands and was directly made in his most beautiful image. God then created the twenty-six angels and gave them names. They would lay down their lives in the name of the Lord, the one true God. God called them his archangels, the Guardians of the secrets of heaven.

One day, God created man and woman, and he called them Adam and Eve. This infuriated the Light. He approached his heavenly father and asked him, "Why create such a creature so much like your true children?"

God said, "My beautiful son, they are frail and needy. They will follow my direction, because I have instructed them not to eat of the sacred tree."

Eve persuaded Adam to eat of the tree because she herself was tricked by evil. Evil had no form or physique; it simply existed, as did peace. All things must alter. The Light found out that the newest children had eaten from the sacred tree. Knowing that his father, the one he loved, was betrayed infuriated him. He raced again to his father. "Father, your frail ones have betrayed you! They should be punished!"

God sat down, peering at his child of light. "My son, what is a fitting punishment for eating of the sacred tree?"

"Death!"

"Oh my dear son, they are mere mortals. They are not gods. They know nothing of what they have done."

"Father, they have betrayed you! They should be punished! They should pay with their lives!" the Light insisted.

God sat there looking at his son. "I gave them a mind to make choices on their own. They had the choice to listen to what I said to them. Otherwise they will be cast out of the Garden."

The Light raged over his father's decision to give these disgusting, helpless creatures choice. He and his father began to argue incessantly on the subject.

God cast Adam and Eve out of the Garden of Eden, telling them that they would have to protect each other and give themselves to each other fully.

The Light was angered. "Why do you give them choices, which you did not share with the twenty-six?"

God stated that it wasn't necessary; they were created to do what was expected.

The Light then threatened to stage an uprising within the bounds of heaven. God attempted to show his son that the children he placed on the planet were doing well because he gave them the power of free will.

The angry son lashed out at his father Physically, but he was no match. God then rose up, angrily shouting at the top of his voice. "I cast you down to Earth, to live among the ones you despise. You will be mutated into a combination of animals. Your job will be to protect them as I have protected you!"

God cast the Light out of heaven. There was an ache in God's heart. He made his son grotesque, frightening, and unapproachable. God had one final comment. "Son, find your heart. Find it within you to understand why I love them for all their flaws and frailties."

Before the Light could plead for his father's forgiveness and for being so forward and bold, he suddenly found himself without his beautiful white feathered wings. He was now naked, cold, and alone. It was dark, and he felt helpless and weak—like his father's mortals.

After waking up on this strange planet, he did not know what to expect. Earth and everything large and small was all his father's handiwork. He was in human form with no wings—grotesque. His body and back were almost deformed. he crawled around in the mud for weeks, foraging for food. He cried out many times for his father. "Father, please forgive me." Tearfully he yelled into the blue sky.

A young girl was picking raspberries off of the bushes and came upon him. She studied him intently, noticing that he barely had anything over him to keep his limbs from succumbing to the elements. She called out to him. "You, come here. I won't hurt you." She had a beautiful smile.

The Light was cold, hungry, and reluctant; he sat there curled up in a ball. She came to him slowly, talking softly, reassuring him that she was there to help and not to hurt him. Once she came to him, she gave him her entire collection of berries. Then she took off her cape off, smiling and talking gently to him. She wrapped him up in it.

A remarkable feeling came over the Light. He felt warm. His stomach was not quite full, but he wasn't as hungry. This young woman sat down in front of him, and he reached out his hand to touch her hair.

Then he spoke. "Your locks are like fire, and yet cool to the touch."

"Oh, you can speak," she said, almost overjoyed. He pulled her into him, and she let out a squeak. This sound was unlike any other he had heard before, and it made him laugh. This bright young woman, with beautiful features almost like that of the many goddesses he had come to know, placed her hand on her chest. "Clarissa. And you are ...?"

He placed her hand on his chest and replied, "Lou."

"Well, Lou, it is obvious to me that you have neither clothes nor food in your manly belly, so if you can come with me, I will get you some warm food and clothes to wear upon your body."

Lou, looking upon this beauty, says questionably, "Why do you wish to help me?"

Clarissa looked upon this deformed man and gently said, "God would not want me to leave you alone to fend for thyself any longer."

Lou, nearly crippled from his fall to Earth, took the assistance of this beauty. They walked through the woods, to a small cottage.

An old woman raced toward them. Lou was weak from hunger, lack of sleep, and the cold temperature, and he was unable to assist with her protection. At that moment Clarissa placed her hand up in front of them, stopping the woman in her tracks. She then began to speak calmly. "Mother, this man is in need of our help. Lest us assist him, and perhaps he will assist us as well."

The weeks were long in Lou's recovery. As he became more and more familiar with this Clarissa, he wanted to know more about her.

One day as they were both out picking raspberries, Clarissa stood upon a rock, looking at him eye to eye and begging Lou to come to her. He complied with her request. Doing anything for her became less and less of a chore. After placing he small-framed arms on top of his shoulders, she leaned in to kiss him. Fire and ice went throughout his body all at once. His feelings for this woman were apparent. He quickly grasped her body, kissing her with his entire being.

Just then, God paused time within this moment of sharing.

"Son."

"Father!"

"Have you learned anything that I have sent you here to learn?"

"I did. I understand how you feel for them." Lou looked at her frozen within that moment, and he touched her long red hair. "She's a vision, Father …"

The Lord looked upon his son and said, "I have given you many gifts, son. I have taught you compassion, love, and humility. This beauty, Clarissa—I created her for you. However, now that you understand why I look upon them the way that I do, perhaps it's time to come home."

Lou stood idle for a moment. "Thank you, Father, but I can't go back home."

The father looked upon his child, knowing full well why he couldn't go home, but he wanted to make sure that Lou did. "Why would you want to stay?"

Lou touched Clarissa's perfect face and her beautiful, long, curly red hair. "Because I would die without her."

God looked upon his son, smiled, and said, "Then you will become a Guardian. Only when prompted or in battle, you will turn into the Guardian form. You will wear the birthmark of the Guardian. Your male children will be marked with the sign of the Guardian as well. However, defy me, and you will be cast in stone."

God gave his son a warm hug. As Lou hugged his Father, he wondered, *Will I ever see my family again?*

God slowly broke their embrace and said, "You will see your family, son. We will be but a moment away."

God then disappeared, and it was only Clarissa and Lou again. Lou quickly embraced Clarissa with a strange new flood of emotions, sadness and happiness at the same time. He began to cry.

Clarissa was no longer stalled in time, and she woke to see Lou tearful. "My darling! What have I done?"

Lou stared into her beautiful eyes. He kissed her deeply, thinking, *How do I make her mine?* Only knowing a small portion of how these beings conducted themselves was going to be challenging. "I am fine, love." He pulled her into his large chest for a moment. "How is it you beings have and hold only one true love?"

She replied, "It is through love that all things are possible. If I gave my heart to many, my love would be weakened by lust or impure desires, or perhaps my heart would be guarded, not allowing anyone to capture it because it was misused."

Lou looked at this gorgeous creature. "I have a place I would love to take you."

Clarissa was nervous but thrilled. "When shall we go?"

"Now. However, I need you to close your eyes, lest my true form frighten you."

"My love, if your true form is part of *you*, then show me. I want to accept all parts of you, even the heinous."

Lou smiled, happy that she may accept him. slowly he changed into the Guardian form. Her eyes grew wide ... and then she began to walk around him.

"I love the way you look," she said, leaning up toward his face. She waved her hand for him to come down to her. Lou hunched over to his beauty. Clarissa immediately wrapped her arms around his strong neck and kissed his lower lip. "Mmm, I love the way you taste as well, my love!"

Lou wrapped her up in his arms. and with a strong guttural, almost growling voice he said, "Let us go now!"

Lou took flight with Clarissa in his muscular black arms, his wings flapping as they took flight smoothly and evenly. They flew to Japan.

Clarissa looked at Lou. "My love, where have we gone?"

Lou sets Clarissa on her feet, "We are at one of the most beautiful spots in the world. This tree is many years old. In one hundred years, she will need support to keep her standing."

Clarissa looked upon this gigantic, beautiful tree. It had long, weeping vines covered in purple plumes, and the way the sunset looked upon it almost made it glow. "My love, this tree is beautiful!"

Lou turned back into his human form and walked toward her. He gently took her hand under the long purple plumes. "Clarissa, you have accepted all that I am. This is the only place that I could take you, where its beauty can only come close to yours."

Lou knelt down. "I must have you for the rest of my life. I don't want you to waste your love and affections on another. Be mine, Clarissa."

Clarissa was wildly excited. She smiled at him and said, "Yes! I want to be yours, Lou! However, we have to receive approval from my mother. Then we could be married."

James attempts to wake me up from this flashback of his parents. "Charity! Charity!" he says. He has both of his hands on either arm, shaking me to wake me from this trance.

Jeannie has never seen anything like this and is extremely worried. "James, what's wrong with her? Wake her up!"

The moments are gone, and I quickly bounce back to reality. I steady my grip on James's arms. I am almost dizzy. "Quick, James, your mother is in the courtyard!"

James looks at me. "Charity, How do you know this?" He's worried and stands still hunched over with me in his grasp. "Honey, are you sure? Really sure?"

"Go, James! Quickly, before whoever took her discovers she is gone and comes for her again!"

James hears the fear and intent in my voice. He quickly runs to the courtyard and finds his mother lying unconscious in the green grass among the bushes. "Mom!" He races down the stairs to the middle of the courtyard. After lifting her into his arms, he notices she smells the same, but she doesn't appear the same. She is different.

He takes his mother into the castle puts her in the great room. I have already alerted Madrid, and she contacts Mr. Angel.

Madrid, looking upon Clarissa's form and the abuse she has sustained, knows knew that Lou will spare no resource to locate and destroy whoever took his lovely Clarissa. "Oh," she says as she shakes her head, almost in disbelief.

"Do you have any idea who did this to my mother, Madrid?" James asks, upset and almost tearful.

While standing back and watching the entire scene unfold, I pull Jeannie back. This is about to get bad—very bad.

I hear the wings flapping and then loud stomping. They are sounds I am familiar with when James turns into his gargoyle form. He has policed the grounds and flown back in. This time I hear almost running from the upstairs foyer.

Lou races down the stairs and into the great room. "Clarissa!" he says as he races to be by her side. He turns her unconscious body toward him and sees an almost elderly Clarissa. Her youth has now faded, and her beautiful red locks are replaced with long, graying hair. Lou leans back almost shock and disbelief, and he gasps.

James quickly walks up to Lou, putting his hand on his father's shoulder. "Close your eyes, Dad. Smell her. It *is* her."

Lou closes his eyes and buries his face in her neck. As he does, Clarissa wakes up momentarily and places her hand on Lou's head. saying. "Oh, Lou. Have you come to save me? If this is a dream, I never want to wake."

Lou weeps quietly. "Yes, my love! I have you. It's not a dream but our reality, my darling. I'm going to take you to our bedroom now, where you can be safe. No soul will harm you again!"

Lou gently picks his fragile, human wife and looks at his son. "You will sniff out who took her. I will give you her clothes within the hour. I am not leaving her." He looks to Madrid. "You will shelter this castle from friend or foe. Anyone with any adverse thoughts or desires will have them known at the door."

"I will need many things for a spell such as that master," Madrid says, worried

"Then get those things you need- -and hurry." Lou turns around and heads toward the stairs. Then he adds, "Because whoever took her probably knows now that she's gone, and they will want her back. They're not getting her without a fucking bloodbath!"

Madrid looks over at me. "Child, how did you know she was in the courtyard?"

I stand there for a moment, not knowing how to say what I know, or how I know it.

"Tell me, child!"

Startled, I blurt out. "God! God said they had no right to take her away from him. He created her for him and no other! So ... he found her himself and returned her to his son."

James stands there in awe. He says, "I have to go tell Dad." He races out of the room and up the stairs, knocking on the door to his parents' room.

His father says, "Enter, James."

James he closes the door behind him. "How is she?"

"She is human, fragile. Alive—for now. But for how long?" His voice cracks, choking back tears. Still, he is happy that he has her back with him.

"I think you should know something that Charity said before she said Mom was in the courtyard."

Lou nods quietly as he starts to take off her clothes and place them in a bag for James. "Charity had a vision? What did she say?"

"She said God said that they had no right to take Mom away from you, and that God created her for you and no one else. He himself found her and returned her to his son!"

Lou doesn't flinch, except when James said his father found her himself and returned her. He looks up at James, tears in his eyes. He stops for a brief moment to wipe a tear from his eyes, and then he continues to take the clothing off of his wife, placing every article into a plastic bag.

James looks at his father, perplexed, "Dad. what does that mean? Does it mean that you are the son of God?"

"Ah, my boy, that is quite a story—but for another day. all you need to know is that I love you, your mother loves you, and you have quite a large family." He pauses to cover his aged bride and tie the plastic bag tightly. Then he stands and hands the bag to James, sighing heavily. "You are so very loved! Now take this. I need you to figure out who took your mother. I don't want you to go after them—I am going to take care of it. Just find out who and let me know."

James looks at his father, who is desperate for answers. "Dad, you are not going to do this on your own. I will tell you who when I find out, but I am going with you!"

"Go downstairs and be with your wife-to-be. Take Madrid wherever she needs to go to get the necessary items to cast her spells. I need you to help protect us."

James sees how very vulnerable Lou is. *What coward would take another man's wife to get at him?* "I will, Father. I will wake them all, and Castle Angelica will once again breathe with the life you instilled upon it many years ago!"

Lou nods, agreeing to wake the "sleeping dragon" and knowing that what they are about to do will lead to immense unpredictability. "Do it after you return."

James leaves his father's room with the bag of what's left of his mother's clothes in his hand. He walks down the stairs, deep in thought. He walks into the great room, where he finds the rest of the group. "Honey, where is Madrid?"

"She went to search through her spell book, to see what she needed."

"Okay, well, we need to go shortly, because when we get back, you're about to see an entirely new side of the castle."

Chapter 12

Lou has taken his place by his wife's side in their bed. She is mumbling in her sleep. Assuming she is finally sleeping peacefully, he finally closes his eyes. He begins to dream of earlier times, when time and life itself on this Earth were new.

Uriel flies to be by Lou's side as he stands watch over their father's holy grail. "Lou! Father is no longer going to associate himself with the Annanuki," he says, a bit out of breath.

Lou stands steadfast with his wings spread out, beautiful and white. His sword is pierced into the ground as both his hands lie comfortably on top of the handle.

"What are you speaking about?" Lou says to his youngest brother in disbelief.

"Father said that they have plans for the human race—plans that Father wants no part of."

Lou, still standing steadfast, turns to his brother, confused. "What plans?"

"They want to take Father's humans and create some hybrid race of them."

Anger fills his chest. Now he has no recourse but to tell Uriel. "Stay here and guard the grail. I will return."

Lou, now concerned for his Father's project, spreads his wings and takes off to see his father.

Lou reaches the kingdom, and his father is sitting within the throne room. "Father! I have heard that the Annanuki wish to destroy your project," he says, concerned

"Nothing will destroy my project, lest they eat the forbidden fruit. I have no concerns, my son," God says, smiling upon his son.

Lou feels even more confused than he did before. "I beg your forgiveness, Father, for I thought that your project was in danger."

"My son, these rare, unusual forms on Earth will not harm my project, because I have created them as a mirror of my image. Their rare, extraordinary makeup will not be able to blend with them." Suddenly it comes to his attention. "Lou, are you not guarding the grail?"

Immediately nervous that he has disappointed his father, Lou says, "I asked Uriel to guard it for a short time. I will return now." Lou bows to his father, his right arm across his chest. While standing, he backs out, turns, and flies back to his designated responsibility.

"Well, what did Father say?" Uriel says with concern.

"He said that he has no concerns. Now go on, find yourself something else to be concerned with," Lou says sharply.

Uriel goes to say something to his much older brother, but instead he closes his well-intentioned mouth and flies away, only looking back at his older brother for a moment.

Lou abruptly awakens to see his wife is still frail. He calls out to his brother. "Gabriel!"

Within moments, Gabriel is at Lou's side. "What is it, my brother?" He pauses for a moment, seeing the look on his face. "What has happened to trouble you?"

Lou stands aside, revealing his once beautiful Clarissa, who is weak, old, and frail.

"What has happened? Is that Clarissa?" Gabriel steps closer.

Lou moves aside, not knowing how to fix this or what to do. He blurts out, "Can you fix her, make her well again?"

Gabriel. looks across the bed to his brother. "I cannot. Whatever has done such a deed has used some very dark magic."

Lou sits in a chair on the opposite side of his bed. He puts his fingers through his hair. "If not you, then who can?" He is frustrated and losing hope.

Gabriel carefully places Clarissa's hand back onto her waist. "Only Father, because only he can give life. I may be able to heal, but I cannot fix the human condition."

"Are you saying that …?" Lou is immediately shocked.

"She is human. Whoever has done this to her did not want her to survive, or to speak of something."

"Of what?" Lou springs up from his seat and paces the floor.

"I do not know, but to go through this much trouble to not only make her human but to age such as this takes a great amount of magic."

"Magic? Who do we know that has the capability?"

"I don't know, brother. You're the only one of us I'm aware of who surrounds himself with those things."

"Is she suffering? Is it painful?" Lou asks worriedly. She appears to be withering away in front of him.

"The human condition is always painful. That's why many cry for Father to bring them home." Gabriel is distracted by something he senses outside of the castle.

"What is it, brother? did you see something?"

"I'm not sure. I must leave now. I can wake her for you, but she may not be herself, so be prepared."

Lou nods as his brother takes her hand and places it close to his chest. He puts his left hand upon her forehead, and he spreads his wings.

Lou stands there, noting his brother's wings and remembering his own. He remembers sometimes how arrogant he used to be at being Father's "first."

Gabriel looks up at Lou. "I remember too, brother. I have missed you."

Lou is afraid to show emotion as well as the deep sadness he holds within his heart. He is punished for a crime to Father he did not commit. He suddenly clears his throat, choking back tears of despair.

Gabriel walks over to Lou and places his hand on his brother's shoulder. "Father will come around. He will. Then when she passes, you will both be home, where you belong." Gabriel smiles at Lou and then he is gone.

Lou begins to cry softly to himself at the mere thought of spending what very well could be eternity without her.

Clarissa slowly opens her eyes. "There's my husband, my beautiful angel," she says weakly, smiling softly and raising her hand for him to hold.

Lou quickly kneels at her bedside, gently holding her hand and kissing it. He cries as he pressed her hand close to his heart.

"Oh, my darling, where have I been? I don't feel so well," she says, a bit confused.

Lou, not wanting to alarm her, with her appearance or what has happened to her, slowly lifts himself. He gently kisses his wife on her soft lips.

"Ah, that's what I have been longing for," she says as he leans back to look into her eyes, slowly stroking her hair back on her head. She is confused and closes her weary eyes. "I honestly don't know why I am so tired…" Her words trail off as she once again falls asleep.

Lou leaves the bedroom quietly and then descends the stairs. He hears voices coming from the kitchen.

"Last but not least, add those two other ingredients, and there you have it: one awakening spell," Madrid says, pleased with her good work. She is teaching Charity how to do magic—well, the beginning steps.

Lou walks in and sees the two women over the stove. Madrid is slowly stirring the pot of liquid. Neither of them notice he is standing there.

I watch Madrid, eager to learn and to fit in.

Lou walks into view. "Is the spell ready yet?"

Madrid is startled at first. "Oh yes, my lord. It is just about ready."

Lou nods his head slowly. "Good, good. We are going to need every reinforcement we can get. I don't want anyone coming after Clarissa. Neither do I want them ruining James and Charity's wedding." He pauses for a moment before leaving the kitchen, "By the way, when you get a moment, ask Edgar if he would be so kind to bring some soup up to Clarissa. Please inform me when you are ready to perform that spell."

Madrid looks upon Lou solemnly. "Yes, my lord, I will."

Lou departs from the kitchen and makes his way back up the stairs to his human wife. While climbing the stairs, he glances at all of the pictures on the wall, when Clarissa was young and vibrant, and James was a young child. He finally walks down the hall to his bedroom. After opening the door, he sees this small, frail figure lying on the bed. Quietly he enters and closes the door behind him, careful not to wake her. He slides into the bed beside her, nuzzling himself close to her body. While resting his head close to hers, he can smell her scent. He takes in a deep breath.

Clarissa can feel Lou lying next to her. She lifts her weakened arm, places it on top of Lou's, and folds her fingers into his. Lou, affirming that this nightmare is actually happening, begins to cry quietly to himself. He holds in his arms the woman he has loved for a hundred lifetimes.

Down in the kitchen, Madrid is reading through a large brown book. This book is unlike any book I have ever seen. It has some sort of strange appearance and looks as though it is leather, but it is not. As beautifully put together as the book, it is also frightening. I ask Madrid what the book is made from.

"What is that binding? It is strange in its appearance."

"Hair, my dear. Hair from the thousands who have defied Lou over the many years." Shocked, I sit there staring. She looks up from the book and smiles. "That was many lifetimes ago, young one."

I look back into her book and suddenly realize that this is some sort of spell book. Curious, I move my chair beside hers. I am an onlooker of sorts, but I'm eager to learn how to protect the people that I can feel are now my family.

I watch Madrid write down many things as she thumbs through the many delicate pages.

"Can I learn too?" I ask.

Madrid looks at me as I sit to her left. She sets down her pen with her right hand and reaching over on my lap, grasping my hand. "I never had children of my own." She gives my hand a small squeeze. "Yes, my child. Yes!" she says, smiling as though someone had given her the best gift of all.

She picks up her pen and begins to write again. "You see, child, in order to wake everyone in the castle, the spell has to be done just right, or there will be grave consequences for all."

"Like what?"

"Well, I could accidentally turn everyone into stone," she says with concern.

I look at her paper. there are many words on it in Latin. She closes the book carefully so as to not let these pages tear or crumple. She places this very strange, very large book back onto the table and rises from her chair. She sighs deeply as she looks upon the words that she has written. "This will do. Yes, this will do."

I stand to join her as she wraps her arms around me, pulling away a bit from me. "We must tell Lou and James!"

Suddenly I get tired and sleepy myself. "I think I have to lie down." I touch my head because this feeling is suddenly overwhelming. I have to close my eyes and sleep right now.

"Yes, child! Lie down on the couch in the great room. I will bring you some ginger ale and something to eat to help rebuild your strength."

Madrid kisses me on my cheek. The babies move, and I feel warmth all over my body. I look at her and say, "The babies loved that!" I muster up a smile.

I walk away from the kitchen table and down the long hall toward the great room. I gaze at the beautiful artwork on the wall. Many, many beautiful pieces of art are hung with great care. After making my way into the room, I get comfortable on the couch, take the blanket that is there, and cover myself with it. I watch the flame as it flickers and waves within the fireplace. I close my eyes as they grow heavy, and I drift off to sleep.

Chapter 13

The Preparation

Madrid walks into the great room with my ginger ale and sees that I have fallen asleep. She places the glass on the table beside the couch and leaves the room, careful not to disturb me. She then walks up to Lou's room, gently tapping on the door to get his attention.

Lou wakes up, hearing the gentle tapping on his bedroom door. He carefully slides off the bed from Clarissa's fragile body. He gets to his feet, opens the door, walks out, and closes the door behind him.

Madrid bows her head slightly. "My lord, I have the spell and await your instruction."

Lou stands against the wall, trying to gain his wits. "I don't want the spell read until James returns. He is on a mission for me."

Madrid is slightly confused. "Will he return soon?"

Lou looks as though he is agitated. "He will return when he has completed what I asked him to do," he says almost impatiently.

Madrid looks at him as though he has had all he can take. she bows her head again. "Yes, my lord. I understand. I will await your instructions."

Lou turns enters his bedroom, leaving Madrid in the hallway.

Madrid understands that Clarissa is fragile, and anyone who has been with the Angel family for as long as she knows that Lou is capable of great evil. Madrid turns and begins to descend the stairs to the long hall, and then she goes into a room that hasn't been entered for a great many years. Opening this door will not only bring forth the entire family and the population of the kingdom, but an army for Lou to utilize to protect the world.

Opening this heavy door takes quite a bit of doing; the hinges haven't been oiled in a great many years. She pushes this door with all her weight, and it opens, creaking loudly and almost eerily as she enters. The room is very dark and has a thick, musty smell.

Madrid then claps her hands loudly twice. Suddenly the candelabras on the walls and throughout the room light instantly. She smiles. "Ah, that is more like it! Now let us get to work."

Around the room are at least a hundred grey statues. She discovers that quite a few have cracked, and some have even crumbled to the floor. She shakes her head, sucking her teeth. She is almost dismayed because she will have to clean up all of the concrete and bury them, as it is the proper thing to do.

Madrid leaves the room to pull the cord in the hall to summon the help.

"Yes, ma'am," a voice out of a wall speaker says.

"Come to the grand ballroom, and bring a hammer, brooms, dust pans, and garbage cans," Madrid says with her thick African accent.

"Yes, my lady."

Madrid walks back into the room, assessing the damage caused by the sudden earthquake that happened months ago. She did not realize then that everyone cast into stone would be as fragile as to crack and crumble.

While walking around the room, she is saddened as to the loss of life. Within moments ten wait staff appear with buckets, mops, brooms, garbage cans, and bags. The looks on their faces speaks volumes; they know that they will be sweeping, Cleaning, and then burying their friends and family. Immediately they begin to sweep the dust into the cans. Some are tearful because they have lost someone special to them. Madrid walks over to comfort one woman who is sweeping her mother up into a can.

James drives up into the garage of the castle. After exiting the Camaro, he stops and leans up against the car door. He looks up to heaven and says, "God, Grandfather ... please, I beg of you. Please do not take my family away from me. My father is suffering. My mother is stricken with something we know nothing about. I'm begging you, please help me take care of my family and Castle Angellica."

Moments later, a bright light appears before him. "My child, I have heard your prayer. Fear not, for I have seen the future," God says in a powerful voice that seems to echo throughout the garage.

James is momentarily shocked. "God?"

"Yes, my child. Protect the ones you love furiously, and the reward shall be for all."

James is unsure whether he should continue to ask questions. He suddenly blurts out, "Will Charity be with me? Will she be safe. What of my babies?"

He is interrupted by a flash of light, blinding him for only a moment. He raises his arm to block the brightness, and then he is left alone. Upset that his questions have not been answered, he goes to walk toward the door leading to the castle.

A powerful voice echoes. "What is meant to be, will be." Then there is silence.

James sighs with a heavy heart, wondering what that means. He is suddenly frustrated and then saddened that he may be losing his mother, and that he may lose his wife in childbirth. Or worse, he may lose all.

He runs up the stairwell to the inside of the house and is greeted by Madrid. "Where are you going, boy?" she asks.

"I was going to check on Charity, and then ..." He sees the look on Madrid's face. It wasn't really a question but rather a request to have his assistance. He quickly recovers his sentence. "But I am going to assist you with anything you need first." He smiles at her as she stands there in the dimly lit hallway with her arms crossed.

"Come with me," she says as she turns around and walks toward the grand ballroom.

James can see plenty of work being done, but he stops short after he discovers that the wait staff are in fact dusting up their stone friends and families. Horrified, he turns to Madrid. "What created this horrific scene?"

Madrid explains in a saddened tone of voice. "The earthquake we had months ago shook the whole castle. Assuming that nothing would ever affect them was a grave mistake on my part."

James sees that Madrid is visibly upset, and walks over to put an arm around her shoulder. "You couldn't have known." He pauses for a moment, and then the thought comes into his head like a bullet. "Did they feel anything?" He is suddenly horrified.

"No. Just the living will mourn their loss. Those frozen will never know they died."

Madrid looks at the severely cracked statue of a woman holding a baby and muttering a small prayer to herself. Madrid raises the hammer, striking the statue into dust and fragments. The other wait staff hurry over to assist Madrid with the cleanup.

Madrid rises up from the floor and says, "Those that have survived this will be here to celebrate and enjoy your wedding." She feels as though this whole ordeal has been bittersweet, and she rises to her feet as James helps her.

Everything is cleaned up. After sighing heavily, Madrid looks up at James. "We are ready. Wake your father."

Chapter 14

Awakening

James walks down the hall. Quietly he creeps into the great room, where I am sleeping. He leans down and kisses me on my head.

After opening my eyes Slightly, I look up and see James. I smile slightly because I am having great difficulty keeping my eyes open. "Hi, baby," I say weakly as James sits beside me on the couch.

James rubs my back slowly and gently. His other hand goes to my belly. I smile as I keep my eyes closed. "I love you so much, James. The babies love their daddy ..." I drift back off into slumber.

James leans down to kiss my belly, Whispering, "Take care of your mother, babies. Daddy loves you!"

He rises to his feet slowly to avoid waking me again. James heads around the corner and climbs the stairs to his father's room. He opens the door and walks in. After he touches his father's shoulder, Lou wakes with his fangs showing and his eyes blackened.

"Dad, it's me," James whispers.

Lou slides away from Clarissa, careful not to wake her. He sits on the side of the bed, reaching over to place the blanket up over Clarissa's shoulder to ensure she will be warm.

James stands there witnessing this, and he whispers to Lou, "Dad, I can only pray that Charity and I have that same love forever."

Lou looks up at his son from the side of the bed, rubbing the sleep out of his eyes. He rises to his feet and places his hand on James' shoulder. "You will, son. You will."

They depart from the bedroom and descend the stairs.

"I assume that Madrid is ready to awaken everyone?" Lou asks as they walk quickly but quietly down the hall.

"Yes, she is waiting. But I have to tell you that there have been some fatalities."

Lou stops and grabs James's arm. "What do you mean, fatalities?"

James turns and looks at his father. "When we had the earthquake, many of them fell."

Lou places his hand over his mouth and then pulls it his goatee. Frustrated, he says, "Let's go before anything else happens, and we lose anyone else."

Lou and James arrive in the grand ballroom. Lou assesses the damage and the loss. The wait staff finish cleaning and dusting. They see their master, bow, and fall into the shadows at the back of the room.

Madrid has everything ready. She walks around the room, placing a cross on the foreheads of those who are not damaged. She then walks in the middle of the room and stops. Lou and James stand in the front of all that are there. She begins to chant.

> Awaken,!
> Sons of Adam, Daughters of Eve,
> Children of God.
> Awaken!

You have work to do! Dawn of the child's rebirth draws near!
Awaken!
The days of Soddam and Gomorrah have come! She will be born to desolate the harlot!
Awaken!
A great beast has awakened!
The children of Christ must be protected!
Awaken!

The room begins to fill with a white light. The statues glow a yellow hue, and they begin to crack at their foundations, revealing feet and legs. Then the concrete cracks and shatter all the way up to their heads. The cross begins to glow a light blue, and then the people fall to their knees. One by one they begin to awaken.

Many are trying to rationalize what has happened. They shake the dust from their hair; each one is covered in a white ash. Then they rise to their feet. Men, women, and children face Lou and James.

There is a slight hum from discrete conversations.

Lou addresses his castle. "Good morning to all my country's men and women!"

James stands alongside his father, stoic with his arms crossed. He is proud to be there.

"As it has been foretold, it has not come to be! Castle Angelica has been under attack." Lou pauses to compose himself. "Clarissa, your queen, was taken and made human. She is now dying of her mortality."

The crowd begins to hum with whispers of worries and anger that someone dared attack the castle. There is fear of the unknown.

Madrid Is standing in the middle of the crowd. she listens to all their concerns, quietly taking inventory.

"You were awakened because the child will be born. More accurately, the *children* will be born!"

The townspeople begin to smile, Clap, and say things like, "That's wonderful! Praise God! The Savior is two!"

After allowing this to go on momentarily, Lou gets the attention of the crowd again. "Everyone will rest until tomorrow." He pauses as he peers around the room. "Tomorrow, we plan our retaliation and how we will protect those we love!"

A man begins to chant, "To Angellica. To Master Lou!" The townspeople join in, and the crowd's voices echo throughout the castle.

James is still standing alongside his father, proud of their people's unwavering love and loyalty to the kingdom. He turns his head, nodding for the wait staff to open the doors.

The doors open, and the townspeople begin to find their rooms within the castle. They hug each other because it has been such a long time since they've had physical contact. Within minutes the ballroom is empty with the exception of James, Lou, and Madrid.

Lou looks to Madrid. "What are their concerns?"

Madrid is exhausted from the spell. "What all of our concerns are, my lord," she says as she slowly bows her head and begins to walk out the doors and into the hall. James begins to leave as well.

"Son."

James stops and turns to his head.

Lou says, "Take Charity up to your room. She is exhausted, and her time is drawing near. Your wedding is next weekend, so she will need her energy to complete her plans."

James smiles, proud of his father. "I will."

Lou walks to the window of the ballroom and peers up into the night sky. "Father, if you hear me, I love you. Thank you for giving me the gifts that you have bestowed upon me. My wife, whom no other could have had a greater hand in. My son: Strong and brave. You made order from chaos. Thank you." Lou continues to look at the night sky, which is clear with many stars. He sighs heavily as he turns from the window.

Just as he is about to walk away, a blue jay appears on the window's ledge and taps on the glass. Lou looks over to see what could possibly be tapping. "A blue jay?" he utters to himself. When Lou approaches, the bird flies away. Feeling as though he is blessed, Lou looks to the night sky once more. "Thank you, Father. Thank you."

Lou closes the door to the ballroom and begins that lonely walk to his room. He arrives at the door of his bedroom and quietly opens it. When he walks inside, he sees Clarissa sitting up in bed, crying.

He quickly walks to her and climbs into their bed. "My darling baby," he says as he wraps his arms around his fragile love. "What is wrong? I was not gone from you that long, was I?"

She lifts her head. "No, but I have a message to deliver."

"From whom?" he asks as he slides a little closer.

"I … I don't remember. All I know is, 'Celeste had to die so that *they* would be born at the correct time.' The twins. They are without limitations. The children part Christ, part Annanuki. Strong. Once blasphemed by God in the original Testament, they are now here to save the world from the evil that has long been foretold."

"Clarissa, Honey, what are you saying? Who was it that gave you this message?" Lou asks as he now turns to her to face her.

Weakening in her words, Clarissa lies listless and agitated. "I have to finish telling you! I don't have much time!"

Lou is upset at the thought of losing the only woman he has ever loved. "Please, honey, don't leave me. I love you." Tears well in his eyes as Clarissa takes her hands to cup his face. gently.

"I love you, my beautiful angel. Oh baby. You will again host your wings!" After taking a deep breath, she continues. "God hast given multiple warnings to change their ways. Fears of great floods, and the warnings, go unheeded. The bastard child will be born. Bathed in the blood of her followers, she doesn't distinguish; she thrives off of the suffering of her own! She grows now, within the center. There, *there*, you will find the birth place of great evil!"

Lou is perplexed and extremely worried. "Are you trying to tell me who it was that took you from me?"

She is weakening and growing frustrated. "I don't know! He told me that right before he brought me home to you," she says as she falls back to sleep.

Lou feels drained and increasingly angry. He slowly slides away from Clarissa and makes his way to the outside patio, closing the doors quietly so as not to disturb her. He walks to the end of the patio. "Gabriel, hear your brother calling you. Please."

Just then there is the sound of wings fluttering, and as Gabriel appears before him. "You called, my brother?"

"Yes. Clarissa has awoken and began to recite the End of Days!"

"Isn't there a blood moon eclipse coming in the coming weeks?" Gabriel looks worried as he walks toward the door.

"Where are you going?" Lou asks.

"I'm going to ask your wife where she heard such a thing!" He quickly opens the door and sees an elderly Clarissa. "She appears worse than she did before brother!"

Lou looks at her with loving grace. "She came back to me, Human, and now it seems as though time is catching up to her."

"Brother, I can't possibly learn anything from her. She might perish."

"Then no! I want every moment I can with her, until…"

Gabriel takes pity on his brother, nodding his head. "I understand."

Lou takes a moment to gather his thoughts. "What are we going to do, if it *is* time …?"

Gabriel stands there staring at Clarissa. She is very delicate and withering away.

"Gabe!" Lou shouts, getting his attention.

"What are we going to do, if it is the End of Days?"

"You realize that we will be under the same stressors that we had a great many years ago. Father left barely anyone alive here the last time."

"The babies are the key to ending the time of tribulations, but for any of this to occur, Charity would have had to be taken by the Annanuki at some point. Her DNA would have to be awakened."

Gabriel stands across the room, now peering out the window. He breaks the momentary silence. "She was. She lived in Wilkinsburg as a little girl. Much evil happened to her at that time. She wanted to scream and alert someone, something, to what was happening—including her abduction."

Lou gets increasingly angry and walks over to Gabriel. Suddenly he grasps his brother. "Are you saying that her DNA was fucked with? She was a baby!"

Gabriel peers into Lou's eyes, seeing the raw emotion he has for her. "She remembers nothing of her abduction; she believed it was men stealing things from her mother in the middle of the night. I saw the whole thing and stayed with her as they took her. They love her—she is their child. They've manipulated her DNA as far back as in utero. She has had many experiences where she 'knows' many things. without being told. She can see and feel death. She has escaped him repeatedly, only to come out stronger. She has been prepared and engineered for what is coming. If it is End of Days, she will know."

Lou lets his brother go and runs his fingers through his hair. "Her eyes are no longer shrouded? She knows *everything?*"

Gabriel looks at the floor now. He nods his head slightly. "Most she knows, but Father had me save her a great many times, until James began to intervene. I monitored them. It was at that time that I saw James so intent on being with her. I knew why Father had me protect her."

"What do we do?" Lou asks.

"Do what you have been doing. It may be she who saves your Clarissa. I must go, my brother. Take heed of everything I have told you."

In a sudden whisper of air and fluttering of wings, Gabriel is gone. Lou stands there, Wondering, *How is it that Charity can save my baby?*

I wake from my nap. feeling still tired and not understanding why. While sitting on the side of the couch, I gather my thoughts, knowing that something is coming. I feel anxious and get up to look for James.

I get to the hallway and look both ways, not seeing or hearing anyone. I head toward the kitchen, looking for Madrid. I push the door open and see no one, wondering at this point where they are. I walk back toward the great room again and reach for the phone to call for James.

"Hey, gorgeous! How is my baby feeling?" he says when he picks up.

I smile but feel like I need him. "Honey, where are you? Matter of fact, where is *everyone*? Where is Jeannie?"

"I took Jeannie to pick up your gown and her dress. I'm already on my way back. Jeannie said that she'll meet you sometime tomorrow."

I'm perplexed and suck on my fingernails. "Um, okay. So you're on your way back to me?" I try not to sound anxious or upset.

"I'll be back there in less than five, baby. Are you okay? Do you feel all right?"

"Yeah, I guess. When I woke up and no one was here, I got scared and …"

He senses exactly how I'm feeling. "I love you, sweetheart. I wasn't gone long, and I just thought that I would take Jeannie to pick up your gown and her dress, as well as mine and Dad's tuxedos."

I am quiet on the phone, afraid to say that not only am I scared but insecure as well. Tino used to wait until I was either sleeping or at work to run to … *her*.

I close my eyes and take a deep breath, touching my belly. "Okay, honey. I love you too, so much!" He smiles so large that I hear his lips actually leaving his teeth to form that grin. "Smiling, baby?"

"Of course. I love you from here to the moon, and back again."

I don't want to have him hang up, but I desperately feel that I should. "Oh baby, that is beautiful. I can't wait to see you!"

"I'll be there in two minutes now," he says, lightly chuckling.

"Okay, bye," I say. I don't wait for him to say good-bye. For some reason, I can't hear those words.

I walk back to the couch in the great room, sit down, put up my feet, and reach for the small throw blanket. I wrap myself up in it as I stare off into the fire for a moment.

Lou soon walks into the room. "How's my little princess?" he says lightheartedly.

I look around the room for a moment, wondering, *Is he talking to me?* "Okay, I guess. I didn't know anyone was here. I was up earlier and didn't see anyone."

"James took your friend Jeannie to the bridal shop to pick up the clothes." He walks into the room and sits in his chair, sighing deeply as he relaxes.

I say anything at this point to interrupt the silence in the room. "James said that he will be back in a few minutes."

"Charity, I was wondering… is it possible that you can have my wife touch your belly and feel the babies? She's not doing so well, and I just thought …" His voice cracks slightly.

I move the blanket from around me. "Absolutely, sir. Let's go." I touch my belly. "Do you hear that, my little babies? We're going to go and see your grandma!" I smile as I slowly walk up the stairs.

Lou hears the word "grandma," and then thoughts begin to rush into his head. *Will she be here when these little babies arrive?*

I arrive at the top of the landing and feel exhausted. Lou comes up behind me and asks, "Are you all right?"

"Yeah. I guess I got a little winded, hiking up all those stairs!" I smile reassuringly.

Lou walks ahead of me and opens their bedroom door. I smell the distinct smell of sage incense. Lou waves for me to follow him into the room. While walking in the dark room, I begin to wonder, *How bad has she gotten?*

Upon entering the room, I see this small-framed, withered figure lying on the bed. I come closer to her, and she wakes up, smiles, and says, "Oh, Charity, dear baby!"

Those are the first words that she has spoken for hours. Lou begins to get choked up while looking at me.

I walk toward her. The closer I get, the more active the babies become. I hold my belly as I continue over to her side of the bed. Clarissa is so withered and old now. This is much worse than I anticipated. I am almost brought to tears.

"Clarissa," I say softly, taking her hand as I sit on her side of the bed. Lou sits in his dressing chair adjacent to us.

Clarissa opens her eyes and smiles. The babies are going crazy deep within me. "Oh, they're letting you know that they are there, huh?"

I smile and say, "Yes, they know who their family is."

While squeezing my hand, she sighs as though she has run a ten-mile race.

An idea occurs to me. "Clarissa, would you like to feel the babies moving? I mean, they are very active right now."

"I would love to!" a weakened Clarissa says, almost excited.

I hold her hand to my belly. A vision illuminates in my head almost instantly.

My tiny baby girl, Aniah, and James Jr. are holding hands. They touch the walls of their placenta. I open my eyes, which are glowing green.

Lou gets to his feet and walks over toward us as Clarissa's body starts to change. The babies are healing their grandmother.

James is just coming into the castle, and he gets a feeling that something is happening. He runs through the halls, up the stairs, and to his parents room. After opening the door, he sees his mother getting better. Lou stops him from coming toward them.

There is a bright light coming from Clarissa's eyes, Nose, and mouth as she opens them and looks up, leaning forward toward me.

A moment later, Clarissa collapses backward onto the bed, but not before a black print appears on her forehead.

Lou gets to his feet, angered and furious. He takes James's arm and says, "Did you see that?"

"That mark on Mom's forehead?"

"Yes! Do you know what that means?"

James is worried about me still holding Clarissa's hand to my belly, and he walks toward me. "No, I don't."

"It means that whoever it was who took your mother was divine!"

"An angel, Dad?" James reaches for me.

My eyes are still glowing slightly, and I step backward. "Whoa!" I look up to James, blink, and immediately get sick. I reach for James's hand. "Honey, I don't feel so good."

James helps me to my feet and walks me around the bed and toward the door. Lou stands there amazed and now confused. "Take her and stay with her. She is exhausted."

James walks me out of the bedroom and toward our room. He helps me onto the bed. I lie down and fall asleep. James lies next to me, touching my belly and saying, "Good job, my beautiful babies!" My belly begins to move, and then the babies go to sleep as well. James, lying next to me on the bed, wraps me up in his arms as I sleep. He kisses me on my head, closes his eyes, and falls asleep as well.

Meanwhile, Lou walks at Clarissa. Her beautiful red locks are slowly coming back, but she is still sleeping. Lou climbs onto the bed with her, still being careful. He looks upon her in amazement as she is still slowly transforming back to the way she used to be. *My beautiful wife.* Lou lies there wondering, *Now that she is healing, when she wakes, will she be human or an immortal once again …?*

Chapter 15

Wedding Day

I wake up next to James, who is still sleeping soundly next to me. I want to breathe in every moment with him, note on every line and crease in his perfect lips. I want to remember how I feel at this very moment. The sun is beginning to shine through the windows. I love the way the sun warms his perfect jaw line, as well as his moustache and goat tee. I pull the comforter up over my shoulder and snuggle into his chest, breathing in his scent. His body is perfect. Mine? Not so much. I am about to burst with beautiful babies any moment now. Still, James thinks I am beautiful ...

I lay there in his arms. knowing that by tonight I will be Mrs. James Angel. I sigh deeply for a moment. James begins to stir, opens his eyes, and pulls me into his warm body, covering me up with the comforter to keep my warmth before he kisses my head softly and falls back to sleep.

I lie there with my eyes closed, wondering, *How on Earth did I get so lucky?* I fall back to sleep, nuzzled deeply into his chest and wrapped in his arms. For the rest of my life, I know with all my heart and soul that I am going to feel safe.

That is something I never felt with Tino, who was all too happy to play the hero to those other women. but dismissed my fears, my anxieties, and most of all my feelings. He never loved me; it was always her whom he wanted. I was the consolation prize. With James, I am the prize!

At nearly ten in the morning, James wakes me up in the most beautiful way. He brings breakfast up to our room with a beautiful red rose lying across the tray. It is a beautiful gesture. I look up at him and his gorgeous body, and I smile. "Hi, baby," I say groggily.

He leans over the bed, kissing my face and then my lips. "Hey, sleepy, are you awake? How is my gorgeous family today?"

Just then, the babies are awake and very active. The sudden flutters in my abdomen make me smile. "Oh honey, can you help me up? I have to go to the bathroom."

"Yes, here, take my hand." He sees how awkward this feels for me and for him too. He puts his arm under my shoulders and his other arm around my legs, and he slowly gets me to the sitting position on the bed. He lends me his hand and helps me to my feet. Then he kisses me, noticing that my belly seems to have dropped. "It won't be much longer now, honey. We'll be holding our babies, and everything will be just perfect."

I look down at his hand on my belly, and then up at him. He puts both of his hands on my face, pulling me gently to that perfect kiss. His mouth is perfect, and his tongue enters my mouth, invading it and making me want him now.

He feels my body language change and pulls me into his body. I kiss him deeper. He starts pulling off my white night gown from my shoulders, revealing my large breasts. He kisses my mouth momentarily and then slides down my neck with his tongue. My clit begins to throb, and my breathing gets faster and heavier. I want him desperately. He licks my neck and comes back up to my mouth, ravaging it and whispering, "I love you."

I whisper back, "I love you. You're the reason I exist." James pulls me closer to him, sliding my nightgown off of my shoulders, which stops at my belly. He gently slides it over my belly, and it falls to the floor. He looks at me, his eyes. black as midnight. I know that he wants me just as much as I want him. He walks me back to the bed, kissing me deeply and passionately. My legs hit the back of the mattress, and I reach back and slide onto the bed. James is extremely excited, and both cocks are fully erect. He moves his jeans and boxers down off of his hips, and they fall to the floor. He steps out of them, sliding his body between my legs. He gently slides into me, and I breathe heavily. It's been so long!

I feel so many emotions all at one time. I scratch his back with my nails, feeling all the passion of this moment. He is taking his time, gently making love to me, his beautiful sexy mouth passionately invading mine. I feel my body letting go and arch my back slightly. he feels my muscles wrap tightly around his girth, and he growls in my mouth.

I feel him about to cum deep into me. He is thrusting into me with more intensity, but he is careful not to hurt me or the babies. His hands grasp mine over my head. I love looking at his sexy body! I begin to cum again; he senses this and cums with me. He stays inside of me for a moment, and then he arches his back, lifting himself up off of my body and being mindful of my belly. I lay there for a moment, and then I start to cry for no reason.

"I'm sorry, baby. I don't understand why I'm crying!" I say.

He smiles at me and slides beside me, pulling me close to his warm body. "It's been a while since we made love, and your body dumped many chemicals into you at the time." I bury into his chest and breathe deeply, sighing and trying to stop feeling this way. He holds me close. "I love you, but we need to get ready. You're going to finally be my wife today!" He says it with so much enthusiasm that I can't help but feel better.

I slide up the bed and look at him. "Okay, baby! Let's get 'er done!"

He puts his head slightly on my belly, listening for a moment. He is quiet, and then he smiles up at me, his eyes tearing up. "I love you!"

I run my fingers through his gorgeous dark brown hair. "I love you with all that I am." Suddenly I feel the urge to cry and to hide my feelings, especially those that make me vulnerable. I impulsively say, "Honey, let's get married!"

James kisses my belly. "Let's do it. I'm anxious to make you mine!"

He slides off the bed, standing there and looking at me. I smile, sliding myself onto the edge of the bed. After placing my hand to my left on the mattress, I scoot a little more to the edge and then get my feet on to the floor, pushing myself up. I am on my feet and waddle to the bathroom to do my business. Then I get back to my feet and waddle out into the bedroom again. I walk toward the dresser, look at myself in the mirror, and sigh.

James sees me standing there and looking at my belly. He pulls up his suit pants, buttons them, and walks over to me. I see him walking toward me. He wraps his arms around me, places his hands on top of mine, and kisses my shoulder and then my neck, "You're beautiful, and you're going to be mine. All mine!"

I smile, looking at us together in the mirror. Then I tilt my head toward his, and he kisses me. I feel the weight of the silence between us and how anxious we both are to be married. Our eyes meet in the mirror. He kisses my cheek and says, "We have the rest of our lives, baby. let's go do the formal stuff."

"Yuppers," I say as I turn around and kiss him quickly on the lips. We both get dressed.

Before he leaves the bedroom, he says to make sure that everything is perfect. "I can't wait!" he doesn't wait for a response and exits. I can hear him racing down the stairs.

I look back into the mirror at myself, thinking, *Oh God, girl! How did we finally get so lucky? I finally have a hero warrior to call my very own! Not to mention, he loves only me, wants to be with just me. I am what he has wanted his whole life!*

There is a knock at the door, and then it opens.

"Hey, beautiful mommy!" Jeannie enters the room, smiling and carrying our dresses. I give her a look, and she quickly enters the room, puts the dresses on the bed, walks over to me, and hugs me hard! The tears begin to flow between us. The babies begin to move around in my belly, poking Jeannie in her own belly as she hugs me. We both break the hug to look at my belly and laugh.

Jeannie leans in and hugs me a little lighter, but she leans back again, holding both of my hands in hers. "You deserve this! You deserve to have a man who will love you for you, and not for any other reason! You're such a good person!"

I stand there, My tears slowing but still sliding down my face. I'm happy yet worried, scared of what is to come. I smile back at her.

She then places both of her hands on my belly, leaning down a little to talk to the babies. "I can't wait to meet both of you tiny babies!" The babies get so anxious when she talks to them. Jeannie pulls back slightly. "What do you say about getting this show on the road?"

She turns around and faces the bed. After picking up my wedding gown, she opens up the zipper and what seem like a million buttons. She places it on the floor for me to step into and pulls it up. I get it on as Jeannie starts zipping and buttoning. We walk over to the mirror to get a better look. I peer into the mirror. "It's a pregnant mermaid!"

Jeannie, being my best friend in the world, says, "You look beautiful, and James is going to love you in this!" There is a long pause as we both begin to soak in the way I look.

A knock at the door interrupts the moment. Jeannie opens the door, and four women enter. They are dressed similarly to Madrid. "Excuse us, but we were requested to get the princess dressed and ready."

I look over to Jeannie, stunned, confused and even a bit weirded out by the "princess" statement. Jeannie being who she is says, "Princess, ha! Well, come on in, ladies!" She winks at me.

I smile as these ladies begin to crowd around me. I am helped to a soft chair in the bedroom that is put in front of the mirror. They begin to comb through my hair with a hair pick; my waves and curls become evident as they begin tying my hair up. The other ladies begin to work on Jeannie's hair too. I look over to her, and she is smiling as these lovely ladies.

They do my makeup, and then they pull out a piece of jewelry; it's old and has a green emerald. The one lady attempts to put it on me, but I put my hand up. "I'm sorry, I mean no disrespect, but I can't wear that. I just want to wear the things that James bought me."

She places it in front of me. "Yes, ma'am." She continues on my makeup. I look in the mirror, and my long curls are draped down beside my face; there are long love curls in the back as well. I scoot to the edge of the chair, looking deeply at every part that these ladies had helped get ready. I say, "Thank you, ladies, for all your time and all your beautiful work."

The woman who wants me to wear that piece of old jewelry attempts one more time to place it over my head. I look over at Jeannie as I put my hand up once again, stopping her. "No, thank you. I have the things that I am wearing. Thank you."

Jeannie stands up immediately, taking charge over this strange situation. "Okay!" she announces as she walks briskly to the door. She opens that door and waves her hand. "Thank you, but that will be all!"

The one helper is still having a particularly difficult time taking no for an answer. I stand up, trying to keep the peace without offending anyone. "Thank you so very much. I feel beautiful! We will meet you downstairs now. Thank you," I say with a confident smile on my face. The woman finally leaves.

Jeannie closes the door quickly and locks it behind them. Then she turns to me with that perplexed okay "What the fuck was *that* about?" look.

I laugh a little. "I know, right?"

Jeannie looks around the bed and picks up my white slippers she bought me. "Here, sit down a minute."

I waddle to the chair again and sit down, reaching backward and trying carefully not to burst a button off of this gown. She kneels down and places the cutest white slippers on my feet. "No one will notice, and you will be comfortable!"

"Thank you, Jeannie. You have been my friend through everything! You've been my rock when I needed one, and now…"

Jeannie interrupts. "Now you start a whole new life, throwing away all the bad!" She helps me to my feet and takes my hand as we walk to the door.

There's a knock on the door.

Jeannie says, "Who is it?"

"It's Madrid. Open the door."

Jeannie complies as Madrid enters the room.

"Oh my goodness!" Madrid says as she walks toward me in my wedding gown. She reaches her hands out, taking both of mine and squeezing them softly. "My, don't you look beautiful!" She has my and Jeannie's bouquets. "Here are your flowers, my child." She hands them to us.

I look at Madrid. She is wearing a ivory gele and an ivory dress to match. She looks beautiful. I smile back at her. "Thank you, Madrid. You look beautiful as well!"

"I have to walk you to your prince, do I not?"

I squeeze her hands, and the concept is becoming extremely real. My hands start to sweat a little. "Yes …"

"Well," she says as she looks at Jeannie and then back at me. "Let us get going then, shall we? We don't want to keep them waiting."

I place my left hand on the banister, and we begin our descent. I can hear the music. *Oh God, it sounds beautiful. I'm not sure what they are playing, but it is beautiful.* As we finally exit the final stair to the floor, the aroma of beautiful flowers fills the air.

We turn the corner together, Jeannie and I, and she pulls my arm slightly. "Wait a minute, sweetie." She pulls my beautiful veil over my face. "Now we're ready."

Jeannie takes to the runner first, carefully matching her steps with the music. Madrid walks behind me, straightening out my train.

Jeannie reaches the front of the ballroom, where she takes her place, standing there with her lovely bouquet.

Madrid turns to me. "Are you ready, my child?" Tears well in my eyes, and I nod. She grasps one of my hands and kisses it. "You will be remarkable!"

Madrid takes my arm gently, and we begin to step toward the runner carpet laid out for our path to happiness. I step on the runner and notice a small pattern of flowers on it. I sigh a moment and continue to walk, looking ahead. We approach the grand ballroom, and there are two gorgeous floral displays on either side of the doors. I look over at Madrid. "Calla lilies! I absolutely love them!" I whisper to her.

"I know."

We stand there for a moment, and then the doors open slowly, revealing what appears to be at least two hundred guests! I gasp, and then my legs get weak. I begin to bite my lip.

James sees me walking toward him with the look of sheer terror on my face at all these people I don't know. He smiles and begins to walk toward me. He whispers, "Focus on me, baby. Focus on me."

I look up and try to fix my eyes on him, but fear is starting to win. My hands are getting sweaty, and my heart is pounding! Just when I feel like I might pass out, James sweeps me up in his arms. "There is my baby! How are you feeling, sweetie?" he whispers to me.

"Oh, honey, I'm sorry. I thought I was going to faint."

Madrid is behind us, carrying my bouquet. She is walking, smiling, and nodding her head at all the guests, acknowledging that she knows they are there. James carries me to the altar. There is a man standing there who is taller than anyone I have ever seen. James sets me on my feet as I look up at this very tall man. He smiles at me and leans down to James. "Are we ready?"

Madrid, standing stoic and proud behind us at the altar, nods slightly at the question.

Gabriel asks. "Who gives this child?"

Madrid steps forward. "I do."

Gabriel smiles as he says, "Let us begin."

James still has a hold on me. "We are ready, Uncle."

I look over to James. "Uncle?" I whisper.

James just smiles as he looks to me and winks a moment. Then we face forward.

Gabriel begins to speak. "Good afternoon. We have come here today to witness a beautiful union. Not of just one woman and one man, but as a family to become whole with God's blessing. Watching this young woman be born, grow, and now marry and become a mother herself has been a privilege.

"James, my dear child, you are so loved. Now your opportunities lie within your union together. To love and to be in love is one of our father's greatest gifts. James, take your bride in your arms."

James wraps his arms around me, pulling me close to him.

"James, this woman is like a flower. She will only grow with you if you give her the essential elements. In order to build a marriage, you must have love. It is the food for the flower to grow. Next, we have warmth and water. Water is life itself. Without water, the flower will wither as the warmth of the sun gives their petals the nutrients it needs. Lastly, the soil. A marriage is based upon a partnership, and the roots of the flower need a foundation. Foundation is understanding, trust, and encouragement. It is through encouragement that the flower will grow beautiful and strong."

Gabriel looks lovingly looks at me. "Charity, this man is a warrior, but like most warriors he needs the fuel to keep fighting. Purpose is that fuel. Every warrior needs to feel needed and have a life's purpose. The warmth of your love is important as even the most delicate of flowers needs the warmth of the sun to stay alive. Sustenance is what both of you must do for each other. Love, honor, respect, be truthful, and always be there for one another as though your lives depend up it.

I look around the room and see there are many tearful people. I can almost feel their emotions. I look back into James's eyes: he looks as though he is desperate to do something. I look beside me, and Jeannie is in tears. I suddenly feel this wave of emotions, and I start to cry. I look up at James for a moment. He wipes the tears away from my eyes so gently and with so much love. I think for a moment, *He is about to be mine, all mine, forever!* I slightly smile as he wipes tears from my face. I honestly feel how much he loves me!

Gabriel interrupts this moment. "Do you have the rings?"

James stands there looking at me deeply. I wink at him, and he snaps out of whatever trance or thought he was stuck in. His brother Jacob steps forward, handing him my ring set. James takes a deep breath, sighing almost like he is holding back. Jeannie comes up behind me, handing me James's ring. I look at this perfect circle and wonder whether our lives will be perfect, or whether there will be many challenges that we will have to face.

Gabriel interrupts my racing thoughts again. "James, do you take Charity to be your wife, your partner in life and the hereafter?"

James states loudly, "I do!" James takes that beautiful ring set and places it on my finger. For a moment I can see him looking for my ring in a store, telling the clerk I am invaluable and he can't live without me. I succumb to my emotions again as tears stream down my face.

I mouth the words, "I love you."

James mouths, "I love you too, baby. Almost done." He smiles at me, again wiping the tears from my face.

Gabriel continues. "Charity, do you take James to be your husband, your protector and partner in life and the hereafter?"

I look up into the eyes of this beautiful man. I say with so much love and devotion, "I do!" I squeak as I place his ring on his finger and sigh, tears still streaming down my cheeks. My voice trembles as my excitement gets the best of me. Everyone in our audience chuckles. I look over and see that Clarissa and Madrid and see that both in tears, dabbing their eyes gently.

The noise dies down, and Gabriel takes another step forward. "Does anyone see any reason for these two children not to be married?"

I got a cold chill up my spine as Gabriel says that to everyone. The room falls silent, other than the breathing of everyone in the room.

Gabriel then says with great pride. "I now present Mr. and Mrs. Angel!"

James quickly grabs me and kisses me. His tongue invades my mouth, taking my breath away. He picks me up into him and then places me back on my feet as the echoes of clapping fill the air.

We begin to walk down the aisle toward the other half of the great banquet room; we are followed by Jeannie and Jacob. We make that long walk, looking at all the faces of those who attended—which was just about everyone James knew his whole life, and all the townspeople.

Many are excited and even happy for us. Then there are a few who … well, to hell with them!

We make it to the banquet room, and James pulls me into his body. He kisses me so passionately that I lose my breath.

Jeannie is so excited. I didn't even notice that she still had my bouquet. I look at Jacob for a moment, and he is staring at Jeannie. *Hmm* … I smile at the both of them.

James interrupts my matchmaking.

"Hey, Honey, please sit so that you can get off of your feet." He really is in tune with me.

"Okay, I'm doing that now."

The next people in the banquet room are Lou and Clarissa. My God, she is looking much better! She almost looks like herself. I am staring at the people as they file into the banquet room. I am growing in excitement. I wanted a disk jockey for our wedding, and we have one of the best. He starts playing some really slow classical stuff, and I love it.

I peer around this room and see so many beautiful colors on the tables. There are beautiful treelike centerpieces that have small LED lights attached. I sigh heavily.

Jeannie walks up to me and says, "What's going through that brain, girlie?"

"Ah," I sigh again. "I feel fat. I'm not as pretty as I wanted to be on my wedding day. I mean, I guess I'm just exhausted with being exhausted already." I smile slightly. She hands me some ginger ale in a champagne glass. "Thank you, sweetie."

Jeannie sits down beside me at the bridal table. "You really have nothing to complain about. I mean, look around you! You have all these people here to see you and James get married."

"Yeah, I know, but I have no idea who all of these people are. I mean, the man doing the ceremony was James's uncle, and I have no idea who is who."

"You have the rest of your lives to figure all that out!"

"Yeah, maybe you're right. Maybe I'm making more out of this. I just want to hold my babies already!" I say, exhausted.

"I know that you do, and I would be lying if I told you that I wasn't excited too!"

James sees me from across the room. He smiles in my direction but is mindful about who is near me. I don't care; I know that I am finally safe here, or just with him. I know that he is going to be that warrior that fights till the bitter end to protect us.

The wait staff start passing out the food. I am so ecstatic to finally be eating. The waitress makes her way over to me. James is now up beside me, and he kisses me on my neck and then looks at me strangely. "What? What's wrong?" I ask him.

"You must be really hungry—I can hear your stomach."

"Yeah, I am." Just as I am about to finish my sentence, they bring me some more ginger ale in another champagne glass; James gets merlot.

"Aww ..." I say because he gets his wine.

"You can have all the wine you want after we have our babies."

I cut into my steak, and it's perfect. I look at James. "Honey, did you cook this for me?"

He grins from ear to ear. "How did you know?"

"Because it is perfect!" He leans in and kisses me again. "Thank you, baby!"

"For what?"

I say, "For making this day special, wonderful, and beautiful."

"I told you that you are so loved, and you have been your entire life."

Dinner passes quickly, and we are called to cut our cake. I look at James. "Please be nice, baby."

He smiles at me and then gently places a piece of cake in my mouth. I nicely place a piece in his mouth, and everyone is snapping pictures. I look at James. "I love you, James!"

"I love you too, baby!"

"I guess we are going to have our dance now."

James and I walk out to the center of the room. They play "All of Me" by John Legend. Oh, such a beautiful song! James pulls me close to him. His arm is behind my back tightly but not too tight; he makes me feel safe and held. I look up into his gorgeous eyes and think, *My God, thank you. You rewarded me with someone wonderful!*

The rest of the wedding party, Jeannie and Jacob, come out to dance with us along with Lou and Clarissa. I look at Clarissa, and she mouths "Thank you" to me with her head on Lou's shoulder. I wink at her and mouth back, "You're welcome."

I run my fingers through James hair in the back of his neck. He leans down and kisses me for almost the whole song. I want so much to thank God for the gifts he has given me. Finally, a man that loves me, wants me, desires me, and always wants me first—I wasn't the consolation prize.

We have reached the part where we have to switch partners. Lou takes my hand as James takes his mother's. Lou smiles at me. "Welcome to the family, Charity! Thank you for saving Clarissa!" he says as he kisses my forehead. I see how much he loves Clarissa, and I finally realize that life is definitely good!

We switch partners again, and this time I am dancing with Jacob.

I say hi and smile at him. I don't know much about him; James says that he is always busy.

"Welcome to the family," he says.

"Thank you!"

Finally the song is over, and James and Jeannie come to me. They both grab me and hold me. James kisses my head and my cheek, tickling me for a moment. Jeannie pulls me into her for a hug.

I see the woman who was helping me get ready for today. She heading across the room and toward me. I am fixed on her; it is almost as if this moment is in slow motion.

Before I know it, she is next to me, James, and Jeannie. "My lord, may I cut in?" she asks.

James smiles at her. "Why surely."

He and Jeannie break away from me, allowing this woman to take my hands. She pulls me into her, making me feel instantly uncomfortable.

I look behind me, searching the entire room for James. He is back talking to his father and mother. After taking a deep breath, I chant to myself under my breath, "I'm good, I'm good."

"My lady," she starts off. "Do you know that everything would have been easier for you had you worn the necklace?"

I peer into her eyes. She looks strange. I immediately grow a set of balls. "I'm sorry, but I have no idea what you mean."

She yanks me closer to her, trying to have my belly in line with hers. I tell her, "Let me fucking go, if you know what's good for you!"

In the next few seconds, I feel the babies move and then begin to go crazy in my womb. She grabs me more intently, and I look into her face. Dark rings quickly form under her eyes, and blue veins fill her skin and face. Her eyes have turned completely black.

I try to pull away as I look back at James. Both he and Lou are hunched over, grabbing their heads; the babies must be sending them a message that we are in trouble. James lifts his head, and our eyes meet. I see the look of horror on his face. He then begins to change. His eyes go black, and he turns full-blown Guardian, as does Lou. I am growing frightened, and time seems to have slowed down. I can see James furiously trying to get to me. Waves of people begin to rush for the doors to leave.

I turn to look at this woman holding me hostage. Her entire face has changed, and her eyes begin to bleed black fluid from them. She then lets out a shrill scream—the kind of scream that a banshee makes.

My ears are now ringing. This feels like it is going to last forever. I think to myself, *Is this what death is like? Does life slow down so that you live your last moments, dying slowly?* Her mouth forms an oval and then grows as wide as her face. I manage to escape her momentarily, however not completely. I run toward James instinctively, and I turn to look behind me. Her entire body becomes rigid, and she looks up to the ceiling. She suddenly stops screaming at the ceiling, drops her head, and looks dead at me. Her eyes are fixed with mine, and she smiles with razor sharp teeth, raising her arm, pointing at me. There is complete silence.

Suddenly there is a large sonic boom! Without warning, her entire body explodes. I am thrown thirty feet backward and slide on the combination of my dress, blood, and meat chunks strewn all over the floor and hanging off of me.

James grabs me quickly as I get horrific pain deep within my belly. I am still screaming uncontrollably while James carries me off in his gargoyle form; this time his wings are fully extended. He takes me into the hallway by the stairs. I look up into the face of James's alter ego. "Honey, my water broke, and I am hurting! Please make it stop!" I say to him tearfully.

Jeannie comes racing to where we are. She looks at me and then asks, "Are you okay, honey are you OKAY?"

I am now bent over. This pain is so intense!

Dr. Seoul rushes out to us. James is still holding me, guarding me.

Jeannie looks at James, knowing what she saw and how quickly James turned into this form. "What the fuck, James! What just fucking happened?"

Dr. Seoul touches James's shoulder. "We need to get her into the delivery room, son! You're going to be a father."

James understands what the doctor is saying. He takes me into the delivery room that they worked on all those months prior.

James takes off my wedding dress. I look up at him. "Honey, she blew up all over me!" He is already starting to change back to his human form while taking me out of my clothes.

I am now screaming for what already feels like hours. The pain is growing with more intensity. Dr. Seoul spreads my legs as James grabs a blanket and puts it over me. I can feel this woman's blood all over my face as it dries, and the smell is nauseating! I scream again as my legs begin to shake. I look up at James. "I think I have to go to the bathroom, honey!" I scream again, and this time I can't catch my breath.

Dr. Seoul looks at James and says, "We're beyond the point where I can give her something to make her comfortable."

James looks me in the face. "Honey. the babies are coming right now."

I am angry as fuck that they are coming right now. "Because that crazy bitch exploded?" I say to him. I am praying that they are wrong.

"I know that you are freaking out and you're scared, but we have to do this now."

I feel like I have to push again. "Oh my god, James!"

"Push, baby. Push!"

Dr. Seoul reaches for a scalpel and gives me an episiotomy. All I can feel at this point is extreme pressure, almost like all the blood in my body has just reached my ass, and there is a constant cramp! Dr. Seoul looks up at me. "Push, Charity. You can do it!"

James lifts me up from my back, crawling behind me on the table and Kissing my head. "Okay, baby, we're going to give him a good one!"

I am exhausted and tired, leaning back into him. "Honey. I can't do this anymore. Please make it stop. Please," I say, crying.

"We're almost there. Let's give him two good ones!"

Believing that this is almost finished, I feel the next contraction coming. It feels like something is scraping my insides like a rake! "Ah!"

James leans me up toward my knees. "Push, baby. Push!"

I am holding my breath. Just then Jeannie catches me doing this and grabs my hand. I look at her, tears in my eyes. "Breathe, Charity! Breathe!"

I catch myself just as she is telling me to breathe. Then I start breathing again. The contraction is over, and I look up at them both. "Please make it stop! I can't do this anymore," I say sobbing softly.

James says, "Baby, I love you …"

Dr. Seoul interrupts. "Here is one of their heads!" He looks up at me. "Give me a couple good ones!" Dr. Seoul can feel that I am coming into my next contraction. "Okay, here we go!"

James leans me forward into the contraction. All sound seems to blur. I am pushing hard and long. I feel something large pour out of me as I also feel another swoosh of fluid.

"I've got him, and they're holding hands! Quick, Charity, push hard!"

I start pushing hard, as though my life depends on it. Then Dr. Seoul shifts and moves the babies around, still emerging from my body. Finally he says, "We have them both!"

Jeannie says tearfully, "They're beautiful! Oh my God, and they are holding each other's hands!"

I lean back into James, Exhausted, trying to catch my breath. It suddenly occurs to me. "I don't hear them! Why aren't they crying?"

James holds me. "Give it a second, baby. He's getting the junk out."

I struggle to catch my breath as Jeannie wraps both of the babies up in the same blanket and hands them to me and James. Holding both of my babies in my arms is the single most beautiful moment in my life. I look up at James and begin to sob. "I didn't think I could love someone so much, and now I know exactly what that feels like!"

James is still holding me in his arms, and cries a little himself while reaching down to touch his son's tiny hand. Junior opens his hand to receive his father's finger. James touches his son's hand so softly. The baby grabs on to the finger that is presented to him.

James squeezes me tighter from behind, in tears at this point. "Oh Charity, they're beautiful! They look just like you!" Then he adds jokingly, "Good thing!"

Dr. Seoul looks up at me, interrupting our family moment. "Charity, I need you to give another couple of pushes."

I look down at him. "Why? Oh God, is there three?"

Dr. Seoul stops my panicked thoughts. "Charity, there is afterbirth, not another baby. Now, give me a couple of good pushes."

I lean and bear down again as Dr. Seoul pulls something out of me. Then he takes the speculum, opening me up a little more. He takes a fine pair of forceps and retrieves another something; I feel it pour out of me.

"Oh god, that felt so weird!" I look down at the precious faces of our babies. I sigh deeply, still catching my breath. "You two were so worth it. All of it!"

Jeannie comes toward me with a warm washcloth, wiping my face softly and getting off the blood and whatever else is on it. She quickly goes back and rinses the washcloth out to bring it back again.

Dr. Seoul looks at Jeannie. "Can you please slide that incubator over here? I need to check the babies' APGAR."

Jeannie complies. Dr. Seoul slowly slides his hands around the babies and then under them, lifting them up and away toward the incubator. The babies start to cry, and then I do too.

James slides out from behind me and stands next to me. "I love you, baby. I have to get Mom and Dad."

I nod as the tears stream down my face. Jeannie comes over and hugs me. James leaves the room, leaving Jeannie, me, the twins, and the good doctor.

I lay back. I don't think I've ever felt so exhausted. I then remember the events before having the babies. "I need a fucking shower! I have to get that bitch off of me!"

"I think we all have a little bit of the bitch on us! Jeannie says, trying to make me feel okay about having entrails all over me. She remains silent for a second. "Y'know, I thought there was something different about her. I mean, the way she kept trying to get you to put on that piece of jewelry…"

I lay and close my eyes to think clearly. "I just assumed that she wanted me to put something of hers on—you know, living vicariously through me."

Jeannie pauses to gather her thoughts. "I am not sure exactly what I saw! I mean, I saw a bright light come out of her neck, and then there were pieces of her everywhere. And then James turned into … I have no idea *what* that was!"

"I know what you're going through. I had no idea what I was seeing either, but these beautiful babies belong to all three of us!"

Dr. Seoul slides the incubator toward the two of us. "They both scored a perfect ten. Do you want to hold them again, Charity?"

I close my eyes for a moment, and before I realize it, I am fast asleep.

"She's exhausted. Let her sleep," Dr. Seoul says to Jeannie. "I'm going to speak with the happy grandparents. I'll be back."

Jeannie stares at the babies and moves toward them. "Hi, my precious babies! I'm your Aunt Jeannie!"

The babies smile and then fall fast asleep, still holding hands.

Out in the hallway, James approaches his parents. "Do you want to tell me what the *fuck* that was, Dad?"

"I am not altogether sure. I think it was angelic, but then possibly someone demonically possessed. Or it could have been a shape-shifter. Then again, a shape-shifter wouldn't have exploded. I'm going with possession."

James says, "What are we going to do about it?"

Lou places his hand on James's shoulder. "I would like to finally meet my grandchildren, as would your mother."

James quickly snaps out of being irate. "I'm sorry. I just think that whatever it was, was trying to kill my family! Dad, I can't go through that again."

"Let's not think about that right now. Let's just get this whole thing behind us."

Lou turns and walks back to where Clarissa is sitting. "Come here, sweetheart," he says as he extends his hand for her to hold.

She reaches for his hand as he helps her up from the chair. They walk behind James and are met by Dr. Seoul.

"She is sleeping. She's had a very difficult day."

James stands there as Lou and Clarissa catch up on the conversation.

Dr. Seoul collects his thoughts. "That odor, as familiar to me as it was, had a stench of sulfur."

James stands there stoically for moment. "How did a demon get past us, Dad?"

Clarissa is feeling more and more like herself, and she says, "Perhaps it was some sort of cloaking spell."

Madrid hurries down the hallway, holding her dress up from the floor. "Are they all right?"

"Yes, for now," James says.

"I must have been pushed out of the castle by the crowds!"

James looks at her questionably but then dismisses his immediate thought. "Did everyone get out all right, or do we have casualties?"

"No, I think everyone made it out. Some are bleeding from their ears from the banshee cry, but that will subside later."

Lou gets everyone's attention. "Today was supposed to be a happy day, a joyous day, and we had unexpected gifts delivered to us! Why don't we all go and see those precious babies."

James opens the door a crack and sees Charity sleeping soundly. Jeannie is staring into the babies incubator. "Hey," he whispers into the room.

Jeannie looks up over the incubator. "Hey, back at ya!" she whispers back.

"My parents want to come and visit."

Jeannie attempts to wake me up. "Charity. Charity ..." she says as she touches my hand and then my shoulder.

James walks in with Lou, Clarissa, and Dr. Seoul. James nears the bed, leans down, and kisses me on my lips and then my head. My eyes open slowly. "Oh baby, I love you. I'm so tired," I say weakly.

"Mom and Dad are here. They want to visit with the babies."

"Oh, okay, honey." I try to wake up more. I slide myself back up the delivery bed and then press my finger on the button to raise my head.

James walks over to the incubator. Lou sits Clarissa in a chair and then sits beside her. James opens the side door to the incubator where the babies are laying. He carefully and gently slides his hands under both babies, who are wrapped in a blanket together. James pulls them out of their warm environment and puts them in his mother's arms.

Clarissa begins to cry while looking at Lou, "Honey, they're beautiful!"

Lou looks up at James standing there in front of his parents. "You did good, boy!"

James is at his proudest moment. He touches his babies slightly on their heads and then turns around to sit with me on the bed. He puts his arm around me, and I get comfortable, knowing that I'm safe in his arms—the only place I want to be. I rest my head on his chest as he gets comfortable with me, kissing my head.

Edgar knocks on the door. "Come in," everyone says simultaneously.

Edgar enters with an extremely large bouquet in a vase. "Please excuse me. This was just delivered for Miss Charity."

Lou stands up and approaches Edgar. "Who sent them?"

Edgar gives Lou a look as Madrid comes in closer to see for herself.

"What have you done?" Madrid whispers to Lou.

Lou replies, "He requested a picture, and I gave it to him."

"May I?" Edgar says as he motions with the heavy vase in his hands toward the table.

"Oh, yes, Edgar, please do."

Madrid takes the card out of the bouquet. "To my beautiful daughter. May you and James have a wonderful and blessed life together. Much love, A."

Madrid looks up from the card, shocked. Lou quickly walks over and takes the card. He reads it and turns to look at me lying on James. "I hope this doesn't mean what I think it does."

"What does it mean, Dad?" James asks.

Madrid walks over slowly, folding her hands in front of her. "It mean just this: Man has no idea that God did forgive the fallen child. Why should he?" she says in her thick accent. "What man don't know is that they created a greater evil through greed, segregation, degradation, and impending annihilation—and it bred something far worse. Many years ago, it was foretold that two children would be born. One good, one bad. The bad would go to many hardships to murder that good baby and its mother before the babies take their first breath."

James sits up a little more now, "What is this evil you speak of?"

"It is man against man. They have learned to stand alone and not together. Trust no one instead of God. Trust their instincts. Satan is a liar; Lucifer and Satan are separate. Man has been taught to believe the wrong things. Now we know that your destiny is far more than what anyone ever could have thought! In the End of Days chapter of the bible, what is right will be wrong, what is wrong will be right."

"What are you saying, Madrid?" James asks anxiously and quietly.

Lou walks up to the babies in the incubator, holding each other nuzzled in their blanket. "It means that your Charity is The One. She is I-Am, a hybrid thought to have been killed off in the floods of Noah. She is genetically perfect for only you, created for this moment to create them."

"So, who is A?"

"A is short for the Annanuki. He is all that was before my father, and he was just as powerful. They both knew that this day was upon us all, however I don't believe they thought they'd live to see it."

"What is going to happen? What do you mean?" James asks.

"Everyone should be afraid. Satan is a liar. He has told them to save themselves by putting poison into their bodies to fight other poisons. Already he's put plans in motion to bond their very lives as currency, blinded them to the very truths that will save the world. Judging by this card and these flowers, I can only wonder how long it will be before the Annanuki will grace us with his presence."

As this story is being told to everyone, I close my eyes and drift off to sleep. James looks back on me, asleep from extreme exhaustion.

"Will he come and harm my family?"

"No, he ultimately is Charity's father. He is her creator. He has long awaited for her arrival. I can only imagine his excitement. Then I can only imagine his rage when he learns of today's events."

As I lay sleeping soundly on James, all eyes are on me and the children. Unbeknownst to the world, Satan's plan is to hand-pick the next generation. Only the strong will survive. The world's number will be "manageable," leaving room for the bringer of sorrow to flood the world with hate and despair. Our destiny and our fight has now begun.

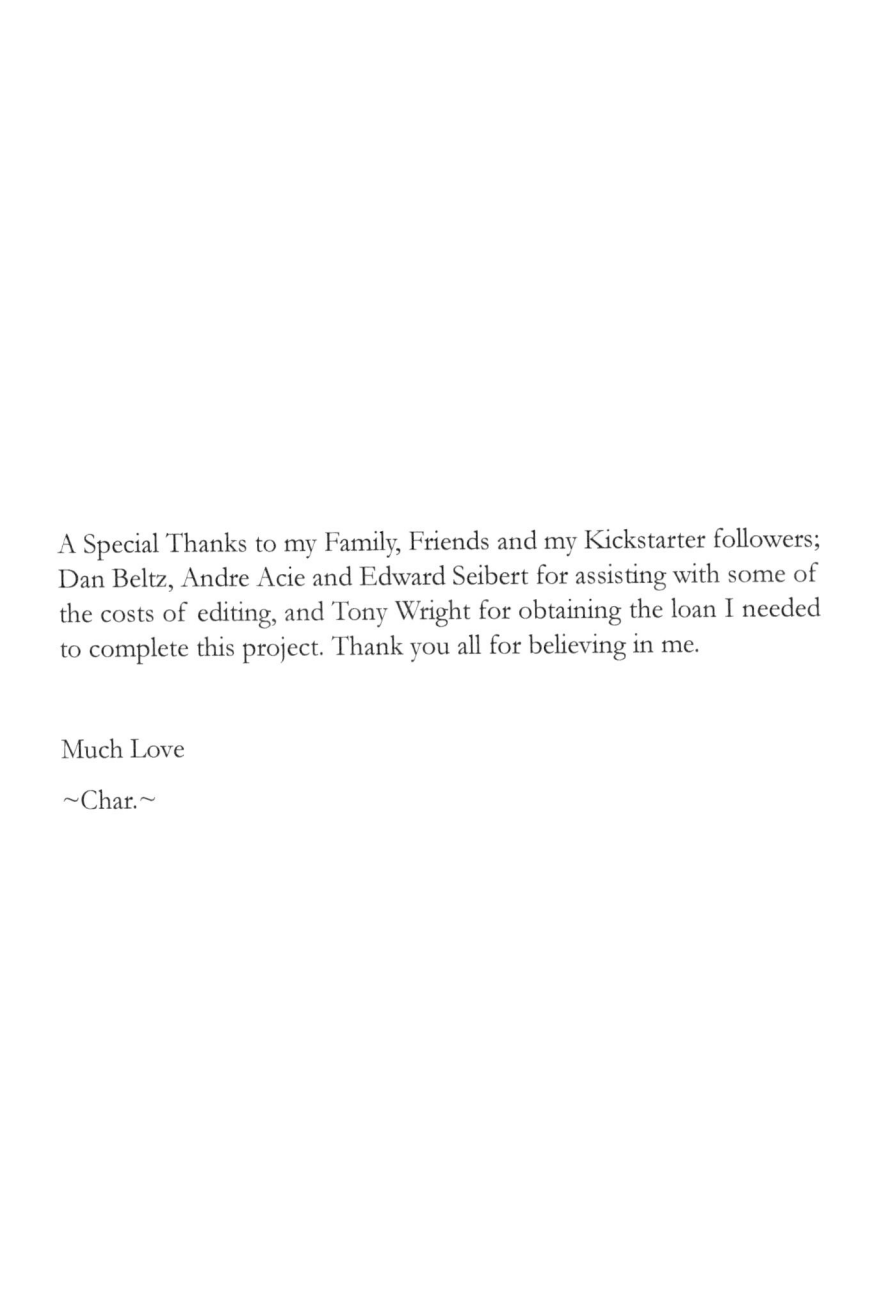

A Special Thanks to my Family, Friends and my Kickstarter followers; Dan Beltz, Andre Acie and Edward Seibert for assisting with some of the costs of editing, and Tony Wright for obtaining the loan I needed to complete this project. Thank you all for believing in me.

Much Love

~Char.~

CPSIA information can be obtained
at www.ICGtesting.com
Printed in the USA
BVHW030851170619
550752BV00007B/41/P